"Zak! Run to the front. Run. Now!"
X-ooming FDR 1933   *Frontispiece (Page 10)*

Time Travel Twins

X-ooming FDR
1933

W. Green

ZIPPY BOOKS®

VELOCITER - SECURUS - ERUDITIO

Time Travel Twins: X-ooming FDR 1933 by W. Green
Copyright © 2016, 2022 William R. Green.

Published by Zippy Books
C222-429-606

Frontispiece Illustration: Lim Yong Wei aka soracilipi

ISBN 13: 978-0-9981623-0-0 (Zippy Books)
ISBN-10: 0-9981623-0-2

"History is more or less bunk. It's tradition. We don't want tradition. We want to live in the present, and the only history that is worth a tinker's damn is the history that we make today."—Henry Ford

TIME TRAVEL TWINS
By W. Green

Saving JFK

X-ooming FDR – 1932

X-ooming FDR – 1933

X-ooming FDR – 1934

Saving Trump

—Zippy Books—

CONTENTS

-1933-

-Chapter I-

-Frozen-

They faced a relentless onslaught of freezing, gale-force winds. Hardened snow pellets whipped into action and stung their faces like icy bees. The incongruous lightweight summer clothing they wore provided little protection. Without gloves, their finger joints wore red bands of frostbite separated by deadened, pale flesh. Snot from their noses congealed, and their ears, dangerously brittle, tingled with pain. The overwhelming and insatiable cold slowly sucked out their remaining body heat. Abruptly, the last twilight silently slid into darkness, removing all hope. The massive storm closed in for a winterkill. They huddled together in a small, rocky recess, shaking and moaning like two abandoned puppies. Their bodies would soon give up the effort. Numb, freezing flesh would inevitably yield. They would die in the middle of nowhere, lost in time and space.

A few hours earlier, they had baked under a blistering New England sun, but now, clad in the same pathetic summer clothing, they desperately hugged each other. Their bodies locked together, trying to stay warm. Speechless and under the spell of the howling, freezing wind, Ethan's mind slowly drifted to thoughts of death. Would he ever see his sister Emma again? She had almost died in the hospital; tuberculosis had taken her to the edge, a place without time. He and Zak were in that same place as something went very wrong with their return flight on the TimeTravelle. They landed in the wrong time and at the wrong place. It was not August 2032, and it was not Dr. Currant's underground lab. But now, this rocky, frozen, treacherous, unknown place made time irrelevant.

Ethan refocused. His fingers felt the back of Zak's head in the darkness, a matted mass of tangled hair and frozen snow. Slowly he slid his hand over Zak's ear, then cheek, until his fingertips found Zak's mouth. He sensed the warmth of his friend's breath. The revelation relieved him, and his strength revived. All that mattered was that they were alive. Finding the other end of the time tunnel was the only way out. They must direct all their energies to the present moment and move to a place of shelter. He shook his friend and placed his parched lips just above Zak's ear. The wind was deafening, and his voice was weak as he spoke. "Zak. We must keep moving. Get up."

His friend stirred and moaned.

"Zak. Get up, now." Ethan extracted himself and struggled to his feet. A tall man, he immediately caught the full force of the wind and teetered. Blindly, he reached down in the darkness, clasped Zak's hand, and pulled. Zak was dead weight. Ethan stepped over the body, grabbed the other hand, and lifted his friend to a standing position. And then he reached around Zak's shoulder, gently guiding him forward as they stumbled into the storm.

"Keep moving. We must find a place to hide." Ethan's words were wasted, lost in the fury of the storm.

The two time travelers trudged forward. Ethan scanned the night for any physical element that would protect them. He looked down at Zak. His friend had his head buried into his chest, and he leaned into Ethan for support. Zak's super-strength and psychic powers were of little use in this environment. They stumbled on, weaving their way through the darkness and cold. Ethan was tiring. They needed to find shelter soon, or they would expire. Incoherent thoughts swarmed about in his head, isolated and flittering like snowflakes in the wind. His teeth chattered. His eyebrows were crusted with the remains of his icy breath. The fingers of his hands grasped each other, seeking warmth that was not there. He could not concentrate. Any moment, he might give up. But then, thoughts of Zak's remarkable intuitive powers popped into his head.

Zak was able to know the unknown. Ethan could not understand Zak's perspective, but he had seen him open doors and create clarity where none existed. He grabbed Zak by the shoulders and shook him violently. Zak's face remained a blank, frozen mask.

"I want you to find a place of shelter."

Zak shook his head. His frozen fingers slowly created the sign for the word "lost."

Ethan read the sign and shouted back. "We're not lost because we're not going anywhere. We only need to find a fallen tree, a cave, an abandoned house, or something. Don't think about the cold. Forget that. Just set your mind. Focus on shelter and safety. Just those two things. Got that?"

Zak took a deep breath and exhaled. A blast of steam billowed out of his mouth and drifted away. He nodded.

"Right. Shelter and safety. That's all I want you to think about. Shelter and safety. OK?"

Zak tried to mouth some words as if he could speak, but his frozen fingers hesitated. Ethan studied the hands. But communication was hopeless. Zak's fingers were now as mute as his voice. Then his friend appeared to drift into a silent trance, not acknowledging Ethan nor the cold and wind of the storm. But he began stumbling ahead. Ethan followed.

Time passed. They wandered. Maybe because he had a purpose, Zak seemed to gain energy. His pace quickened. They headed straight into the driving wind.

"Do you feel it, Zak?"

Zak did not pause. They continued their desolate march in the driving snow for a few more minutes. Zak stopped abruptly, and Ethan almost stumbled into him. He held onto Zak's shoulders to ensure they would not be separated. Zak straightened up and then seemed to point his chin to the right. His eyes looked up through the snow as if he could see the stars. He made a loud guttural sound and headed off rapidly, with Ethan tagging along, his hands clinging to Zak's shoulders. Soon Ethan sensed a diminishment in the wind and a quieting of the storm. It almost felt warmer. He knew that was impossible, but it gave him hope. They walked together now with purpose, stride for stride, like one animated being. Twenty more paces, and the wind had died down. It felt peaceful. Five more steps, then they hit a wall of stone.

Zak waved his arms up and down and then reached out to touch the face of the rock wall. He slid to the right, both hands touching the wall as he traversed.

Ethan followed. Disengaged from Zak's shoulders, with his friend only a few feet ahead, Ethan struggled to see Zak's shadowy form, a black ghost creeping through the night. Then the apparition disappeared. Zak was gone. Ethan pushed ahead, his fingers sliding along the ice-cold granite. "Zak," he called out. "Where are you?"

Ethan's probing hands found nothing as he stumbled forward. Then he lost his balance and fell into a void. Time froze, and he awaited his death. He hit the ground, a short but frightening fall onto soft dirt. He gasped for air and cleared his head. The smell of pine needles filled the air. The storm had disappeared, and now he was enveloped in luxurious quietude and relative warmth. He called out to his friend but only heard the distant sound of the wind rushing past the rock opening above. Then a scratching sound and the space erupted into a blinding fireworks display. After the initial blast of light, Zak's face was visible. He wore an impish grin and held a lighted match in his hand. Then he produced a crazy, almost maniacal sound reverberating off their shelter's stone walls.

In different circumstances, Zak's unusual outburst might have frightened Ethan. But now, he just laughed. For a moment, the time travelers marveled at the tiny flame until their instant outbreak of joviality died along with the match.

"Zak. Another. Do you have another match?"

Silence and blackness filled their frozen tomb.

"Wait! I'm sitting on pine needles." Ethan cupped his hands and drew in the forest droppings to create a flammable mound.

 Zak's new match popped, and everything glowed brightly. Zak carefully moved it to light the needles. Slowly, one by one, the little brown firesticks absorbed flame. Gradually they combined to form a small fire. Ethan sprinkled clumps of the new combustibles onto the building blaze.

Zak held his hands close to the fire. He rubbed them together and tested their flexibility by wiggling his fingers. He smiled as he looked up from his hands.

Ethan smiled too. His frozen face didn't allow for much of a grin, but it was enough to make Zak chuckle. "What's the joke?" he asked.

"Your face," Zak signed. "You look like a snow monster."

"Ah. The comedian is back. You're talking again. That's good. The old fingers are back in action. I missed that." He glanced down at the fire. "Hey, let's build this fire before it goes out."

They found scattered twigs and small branches nearby and used them to tweak the fire. Slowly, it grew into a real fire. Zak looked up at the night sky above them, and Ethan's eyes followed. Only a few flakes of snow filtered down into their hidey-hole. The storm was abating. The flickering light of the fire rippled the jagged edges of the opening against the blackness of night beyond. As if they made a silent pact to ignore their plight, they looked down again and focused on the fire between them. They sucked in its warmth, which made life possible and sat transfixed by the fire's hypnotic dance for minutes, drifting into a hazy dream world of exhaustion and sleep.

Ethan was the first to shake it off. "Wake up."

Zak stirred.

Ethan rekindled the fire, and it glowed brightly. "We're not out of the woods. We've got to find a way out. There's enough stuff down here that we can burn to keep the fire going if we sleep in two-hour shifts. Maybe in the morning, we'll have enough light to explore. OK?"

Zak nodded.

"I'll take the first shift." Ethan dug into his hidden pants pocket, and his fingers found his antique railroad watch. "According to this, it's 3:21, whatever that means. But I'll set it to 5:30 and wake you in two hours. Now get some sleep."

Zak needed no encouragement. He curled into a ball close to the fire and was asleep in seconds.

The rhythmic sound of Zak's heavy breathing, the crackling of the fire, and the wind rustling above filled the stone pit and was hypnotic and comforting to Ethan. He nurtured a hope that he and Zak would somehow make it back to Mystic Heights in 2032.

-Chapter II-

Attacked

Ethan's thoughts rippled up like gentle waves lapping at the shore of reality. His eyes blinked. He was awake, but he didn't move. He stared at the bright oculus above. In time, his vision accommodated the blast of daylight. As he struggled to get his bearings, he gazed at the rocky confines of their prison. The cold permeated the cave and his being. The remnants of last night's fire smoldered dumbly. Zak was curled into a tight ball, his body vainly attempting to preserve heat.

First things first, Ethan thought. The fire had died. Last night's irrepressible need for sleep had overcome his reasoning. He remembered battling the urge to sleep, but he drifted into sleep a few minutes before his shift ended, allowing the life-preserving flames to die. Zak had been no help. He never awakened. Ethan tossed pebbles at him one by one, and Zak weakly swatted at them as if they were pesky flies. One bounced off his nose. He groaned. Opening his eyes, he gazed at Ethan and signed his disapproval with profane and universal single-finger talk.

"Same to you, Sleeping Ugly," replied Ethan as he babied the fire back to life.

Zak spoke. His hands and fingers moved slowly and deliberately, "*You fell asleep?*"

"Hey, I made it about an hour and 45 minutes. You slept the entire night. Anyway, I'll get the fire going again. So we won't freeze." Ethan shuffled about, gathered tinder, and soon restored the blaze. "Are you OK?"

Zak nodded and looked up at the sunlight streaming through the rocky opening above. "*At least the sun is out. We'll make it, Ethan. We just need to get out of here.*

Figure out where we are. What time it is, and how to get home. Right?"

Ethan didn't answer. He focused on the sunny window to the world above, a cloudless blue sky taunting him. He wondered how they would get out of the pit. The edge of the opening they had fallen through was about ten feet above. Maybe if Zak stood on his shoulders, he could get a handhold and pull himself out. Or perhaps they could find a ladder, a rope, or something. In that instant, he squinted to see more clearly. Something above caught his attention, flickering and dancing in the harsh glare. It was difficult to read its size or shape. It jumped about like a large horsefly. "There's something up there, Zak," he said softly.

Zak looked up and studied the view. He shielded his eyes. Then he shrugged his shoulders. *"Just a bug."*

"Wherever we are, it's winter. No bugs." Ethan stood, and his six-foot-five two-hundred-twenty-pound frame filled the space above Zak and shaded him from the glare.

Zak's face changed instantly from a look of inquisitive wonderment to a fearful concern. Quickly, he signed one word to Ethan, *"Drone."*

Ethan whispered, "Get up slowly. Grab a burning stick, and let's move deeper into the cave." He looked up again just as the midget drone rose higher and seemed to disappear. "Let's go. It's gone away."

They ran back into the cave. Thirty paces in, the natural cavern funneled into a dead end. Their burning sticks provided just enough light to make them realize they were trapped. There was no exit, and although the opening in the front of the cave might offer the potential of escape, it appeared to be guarded by a drone. Breathing was difficult. Aside from the terrible tension, the air was heavy and stale. Both hunched over. Their make-do torches were dying out.

Neither moved. Zak looked at Ethan and elbowed him gently. His eyes revealed he sensed something nasty coming. Ethan was aware that Zak sometimes knew what couldn't be known, and that thought scared him. Ethan looked back toward the cave opening. Nothing, no sounds, no movement, no shadows. Then he heard a buzzing, whirring, awful sound, like flies swarming a moldering corpse.

The noise reverberated in the confined space. Zak and Ethan inched backward, all the while searching for the source. Then, through the smoke and haze that filled the cave, they saw them. Dozens of dragonfly drones hovered in an undulating dance about twenty feet distant, their wings sparkling iridescently in the shaft of sunlight.

Ethan had never seen a formation of drones. Occasionally, at home, he would spot an isolated drone, an artificial dragonfly, bee, or hummingbird in the garden mixing with natural insects and birds. This government spying had been going on for years, and everyone was accustomed to the concept. The drones were like a cop on a beat, a symbolic representation of a system that taunted the public's awareness with ever-present, all-seeing eyes and ears. But never before had he been frightened by them. Now he sensed a threat beyond privacy intrusion. This squadron of bugs looked lethal. He had heard stories that such weapons existed. They were employed for crowd control and sometimes as stinging killers.

The first wave of a dozen drones split off from the group. The buzzing sound increased and signaled their impending attack. "Here they come!" shouted Ethan. "Get behind me and face away. Use two hands to crush them if you can."

Immediately, Zak took a rear position facing the cave's back wall, tight to Ethan's body. The dragonflies moved in quickly. Half of them attacked Ethan. The remainder flew around both sides of him and went for Zak. The first drone to strike caught Ethan in the left eye. Another flew into his right eye. Ethan thought they were attempting to blind him. He swatted at them viciously and crushed one on his forehead. Behind him,

Zak grunted and groaned. Back to back, they bumped into each other as they flailed fiercely.

The first squadron had stayed above their waists. Ethan guessed they could do no great harm unless they landed on a skin surface. "Keep at it, Zak. Keep beating them. Crush them!"

Then the second squadron attacked the lower portions of the two bodies. While Ethan couldn't see these new enemies, he sensed them curling around his ankles, looking for soft tissue. Then they bit. An electrical charge surged into his leg. The shock continued for a few seconds. Then two more bites. Ethan bent over to clear his ankles, slashing at them wildly. He heard the crunch of destruction as his big hands whacked bug after bug. Then he felt them on his neck—zap—zap—zap. The volley of bites stole his will to fight. His body was rife with pain. They attacked his crotch. He swung savagely, beating everywhere. He was possessed with survival. But he knew they would lose. There were too many, and each bite weakened him more. His muscles became rubbery. "Zak! Run to the front. Run. Now!"

Ethan took off toward the bright daylight at the front of the cave, and Zak and the dragonflies followed. They flew faster than the men could run. Under the cave entrance, the buzzing mass regrouped. The drones swarmed, circling for a final attack. Ethan looked at Zak and saw bloody bite marks on his friend's face. Zak looked dazed; his movements were languid. Ethan knew they wouldn't survive another attack. They were exhausted. Their eyes met, and Ethan wondered if this was the end.

Amid the buzzing clamor, he heard a voice from the back of the cave. It was deep and commanding but muffled. "Drop to the floor. Now!"

They followed orders. Ethan first, then Zak, who fell atop Ethan's prone body. Seconds later, they felt the presence of another. Someone stood astride them, his well-worn, black hiking boots inches away. Ethan looked up at a tower of a man. Bearded and red-faced, he wore yellow goggles with a built-in headlamp and a filter mask over his nose and mouth. His clothing was a tight-fitting, lightweight, green-and-tan two-piece camouflage outfit with a tool belt. The holstered revolver also caught Ethan's attention.

His right hand held a red-and-white tubular object. It looked like a can of spray paint, but Ethan was in no mind to be an observant witness. He was in severe pain. The electric shocks had weakened his ankles, and the attack on his neck and ears had left him with crawling, painful nausea.

Above, the drones regrouped and swarmed in place as if the intruder's presence had confused them. Self-governed, their program recalculated. This time, the entire force of drones, which had been reduced by the earlier defensive actions of Zak and Ethan to about twenty, swooped down wing-tip to wing-tip and headed for the bearded man's head. But before they could get within three feet of their target, the man aimed his spray can and blasted a continuous sweeping translucent mist. The drones flew into the fog, fluttered, pivoted, and rained down. One landed on Ethan's forehead and bounced to the ground. There was still some life left in the tiny beast. It struggled to move its wings, but they were stuck to each other with a thin layer of glue. It pulsed and gyrated for a few more seconds and then stopped moving.

Ethan's poetic close-up view of the death of the winged machine was interrupted by a boot that stepped on the creature and crushed it into the cave's stone floor. The man stomped on every drone, methodically grinding them into oblivion. He removed his mask, clicked it onto his tool belt, and slid away into the cave's depths. As he ran through the darkness, the light from his headlamp weaved and bobbed on the rocky walls. He stopped at the back of the cave and rammed his heel down on each of the drones knocked out by Zak and Ethan earlier.

"Die, you bastards!" he shouted.

The ground near Ethan and Zak was littered with dead dragonflies.

"Up!" shouted the man.

Zak and Ethan slowly arose. Adrenaline returned to its sources, leaving behind two shaking and weakened bodies. Zak's movements were slow. Ethan felt no better, barely able to move. The aftereffects of the electrifying drone attack lingered on.

"Get your butts moving if you want to live. More coming. They've got our number now. There's no end to these buzz-bots. We pissed 'em off." He lumbered deeper into the cave. They followed closely behind.

"What did you spray them with?" shouted Ethan as he tried to keep up.

The man looked back. "Artist's spray-mount. Blinds 'em and glues their wings together. Works great on a small bunch, but you'll die if they come at you hundreds at a time." Then he reached into a pocket and extracted a mass of dark brown fur with a long naked tail, a dead rat. He tossed it past Ethan and Zak toward the cave entrance. The bearded man looked at Ethan and laughed. "Just buyin' some time. It confuses the drones. They're suckers for freshly killed meat."

"Right," mumbled Ethan.

Zak smiled. He appeared much stronger now and seemed to enjoy their strange savior's bizarre antics.

"Got to go. They don't give up."

"Where?" asked Ethan. "This place is a dead end." His words echoed off the walls of the narrowing cave.

The bearded man looked up. His light illuminated the knotted end of the climber's rope, which dangled down from a small hole in the cave ceiling. "You go first," he spoke to Ethan. "Your friend and I will give you a boost."

Ethan grabbed the end of the rope without thinking while the man crouched in front of him. "Help him climb up my back," he demanded of Zak. Ethan pulled himself up as Zak positioned Ethan's feet first on the man's back and then on his shoulders. Ethan rose a few feet through the rocky hole.

"You're next," said the man to Zak. "Grab the rope, and I'll push you through."

Zak didn't need the man's help. Shorter than Ethan by a half-foot and weighing fifty pounds less, Zak went up hand-over-hand quickly, and Ethan hauled him in. Breathing heavily, they both peered over the opening. The man's bright headlamp glared at them. Reflected light exposed a smiling bearded face.

"Wow. You're a strong little mother. You climb like a monkey in heat." He grabbed the end of the rope. "OK, guys. You haul me up and get my ass out of here."

Ethan and Zak pulled. The man was heavy, but the time travelers had recuperated much of their strength. Ethan marveled at Zak's super-strength as they reeled in the man. In the end, Zak did most of the heavy lifting. Ethan reached down to grab the newcomer's belt. He hauled him through the opening.

The man wasted no time. "Help me slide the stone into place," he demanded. It was a roughly round stone, a few inches thick. The top was smooth, but the bottom had rugged features. The three strained and slid it into position. It dropped into a tooled recess with a thud, closing off the opening. "Let's go. We need to get our body signatures out of here.

-Chapter III-

Revelation

Five minutes of challenging travel on the undulating and twisting rocky trail ended when their leader stopped dead in his tracks. He turned to face them, unbuckled his tool belt, and dropped it. The gun remained in his waist holster. He sat on a boulder and removed his goggles and headlamp. He positioned the light on the ground, pointing it toward the cave's ceiling. A white ring of illumination radiated above. Zak and Ethan took his cue and flopped down on the cave floor facing him. Breathing heavily and sweating, Ethan was pleased to take a break. No words had been spoken during their escape. Now they sat listening to their own heavy breathing echoing off the walls. After a few seconds of silence, Ethan coughed and cleared his throat.

"There's a water bottle on that tool belt," said the man. "Welcome to it."

Zak reached out, removed the water bottle, and took a quick swig. He passed it to Ethan, who drank heartily.

The bearded man seemed to enjoy it all. He smiled and nodded. "So, the big guy's thirsty. How long were you guys trapped in that cave?"

"We fell in last night," answered Ethan.

"Why the hell were you out last night in a blizzard? Wearin' those clothes?"

Ethan smiled. "That's a good question. We were lucky to drop in."

"Maybe. You never know." His voice was emotionless.

Ethan couldn't determine the man's intentions. He thought he would try a friendly approach. "Ethan's my name. And this is Zak."

The man looked at Zak for some kind of response. Zak looked at Ethan.

"Zak can't talk without his *Voicenator*. It got lost in the storm. He uses sign language."

The bearded man shrugged his massive shoulders and looked at Zak. "Got it. No biggie. Most people talk too much anyway. I'm called Vali."

Zak signed to Ethan. *"Tell him we got left behind on a school excursion. We got off the bus for a break, and they left without us."*

"What's he saying?" Vali rippled his fingers through his long matted hair and stretched. Ethan noticed his hands, arms, and neck were covered with tattoos. One of them read *MOM SUCKS*. His eyes darted back and forth; their enormous, deep-set pupils gave his ruddy face an unnatural look of friendliness—a rosy, doe-eyed giant. But now, those eyes narrowed in skepticism.

Ethan thought for a moment. "Zak wants me to thank you for saving us from the drones."

"Can't talk, huh?"

"No. He's a slightly defective first adopter in that 'Employ America' program. You know, 'Creating perfect people for the perfect job.'"

"Yeah. I remember that program. MOM was testing out her equipment. Creating beautiful people. The sheeple loved that idea." He looked at Zak. "Well, except for those drone bites, he's a good-looking hunk of a man. He could even model for a propaganda poster as the ideal twenty-first-century American male." He laughed, exposing a rotten set of yellowed teeth. The man noticed Zak's reaction. He bent over and leaned in at them one by one. "Pretty ugly mouth, huh? Well, that's what happens when you live underground for nine years."

"What do you mean?" asked Ethan.

Vali leaned back, straightened up, and placed his right hand on his holstered revolver. "At the moment, my friends, I ask the questions. Tell me a story. And it better be good. We don't like visitors down here."

Ethan took a breath and cleared his throat. He wanted to be convincing. They had no idea where they were. They weren't even sure what year it was. They knew nothing about the man with the gun. What or who he represented was unknown. But he might be their best chance to get home. One more deep breath, and storyteller Ethan was on his way. "Well, we're students at Cordwell University." He swallowed and paused before proceeding, looking for Vali's reaction to the name, but there was none. "Uh. We were on a field trip for a natural science class. You know, geological formations, lithostratigraphic units. School stuff. Anyway, we got off the bus to stretch our feet, and Zak and I drifted away from the group. Then we saw a strange animal. Looked like a cross between a goat and a cocker spaniel. We chased it into the woods, lost it, and when we got back, the bus was gone."

Vali smirked. "And you dressed like that for a field trip. Those are weird-looking clothes."

Ethan ignored the comment about their 1930s-style clothes. "I know it sounds stupid, but we left our jackets and boots on the bus. It was supposed to be a quick stop, but it turned into a nightmare."

"Cordwell. That's Mystic Heights, right?"

Zak and Ethan both nodded. Ethan was pleased that the man appeared to be buying the story.

Then Vali stood up and towered over them. He lowered his chin and stared through them. "We're miles from Mystic Heights. Are you telling me you somehow crossed the border? Walked through a blizzard? In those clothes? All the way up here? Then just dropped into the cave entrance? Sounds like a load of crap to me." His hand again rested on his holster. "Who are you guys?"

No one spoke. Sounds of water slowly dripped, reverberating off the walls. Ethan's mind raced. He had to come up with another story. "OK. Truth is, we were on a mission but not related to school. We wondered what was on the other side of the border. We rode out to the edge on our hoverboards. It was late afternoon. We got near the border, but we never crossed it. We were just looking for a little excitement. We did go in the woods, and we did stop for a break." He made a face and shook his head. "No strange animals. But then we were ambushed by a gang of nasty, ugly people. They took our wheels, jackets, hats, and gloves and took off. After that, we just walked. We must have stumbled into some kind of electrified force field fence. Maybe it knocked us out. Something happened. We don't know what. Then it got cold. We were in a blizzard. We wandered in the darkness for hours until we fell into the cave. Then you and the bastard bugs found us."

Vali just stood tall and digested the story. "So you're pampered college boys. Mystic Heights. I hear that's a special place. And you knew nothing about the outside world. So you were curious about what's on the other side."

"We were," said Ethan, "and we still are."

Vali laughed. "Well, you two are the luckiest mothers I've run into in a long time. Mystic Heights. Some kind of research and development town. So they say. A plush training ground and reservation for the semi-chosen."

"Well, we don't know about that. We really don't know much other than what we've been told. We're happy with it. Not wild about the lack of privacy. But that's the way things are. As they say, it's for our protection. We know about the outside world from watching television. It looks a lot less desirable than Mystic Heights. Very dangerous. Nobody's allowed out except on special business. My father was an exception. He traveled out quite a bit, but he did things for the government. He was knocked out of commission years ago. He's well now. But he doesn't leave town anymore."

"So your father's a Fed?"

"No. He was on contract. Private. But he's retired now."

"Right." Vali huffed. "And what are you two going to be when you grow up?"

Ethan thought for a moment. "After we graduate, we'll be assigned a career path based on our strengths and skills."

"And everyone will live happily ever after. Sure. You know who's coming to town real soon? Don't ya?"

Ethan shrugged his shoulders.

"Santa Claus," replied Vali. His laughter filled the cave. When he stopped laughing, he spoke again. "Let's get moving. I've got some things to show you. It might expand your college-boy minds a bit. You two look pretty smart. But really, you know nothin'."

Zak and Ethan looked at each other for support.

Vali stood and donned his gear, and they took off again, following him deeper into the cave.

Their journey continued, sometimes requiring them to crawl through narrow fissures while other locations broadened into little caverns. Even though Zak and Ethan were in excellent physical shape, the rigors of time travel, their battles with the storm, and the drones weakened them. The knees of their pants were worn through, their fingers were cut, and sweat soaked their shirts. Several times they asked Vali to stop. He seemed to operate almost effortlessly, and he complained at every request. They rested again. Fortunately, he carried food sticks and water, which he shared. While eating, Ethan pulled out his antique railroad pocket watch to check the time. It was approaching two in the afternoon.

"Nice machine. Does it work?" asked Vali. He extended his hand.

Ethan handed over the pocket watch. "Gold-plated. It's a railroad watch. Belonged to my great-great-grandfather. It's old, but it keeps time to the minute."

Vali examined it closely. "Very nice." He smiled. Three words popped out of his rat's nest of yellowed teeth. "I'll take it."

"What do you mean?"

"I mean, I need it. I'm underground. It's dark in these caves. Get it? No sun. I need to know the time. All those battery-operated watches aren't worth a crap. I can't get new batteries. I need this watch."

Ethan was perturbed. "I get that. But it's mine."

Vali smiled again. "Consider it my fee for saving your butts. You think you'd ever find your way home on your own?

Ethan looked at Zak, who signed back, "*The man has a point.*"

"OK. The watch is yours. Enjoy."

Vali nodded. He pulled a beat-up black plastic watch from his jacket pocket and used it to set the new one. Then he placed both in his zippered pocket.

"When do we get home?" asked Ethan.

"Well, we need low tide." He pulled a small leather-bound booklet out of his pocket and flipped through the pages. Finding the correct page, he strained to read it, then lifted his head to speak. "Looks like we'll catch that in about three hours." He tapped the booklet on his hand and then returned it to his pocket. "We have to cover some ground. And you have something to see. Let's go."

The trail led downhill now. Twenty minutes later, they entered a new space. "Where are we? Looks like it's man-made. Is it?"

Vali didn't stop to respond. He and his headlamp moved ahead into the new area. "You're right. We're entering part of an abandoned mine. Lead or copper. This thing's been around for a hundred years. Anyway, the trail gets easier."

He was right. They made good time now on the downhill and flatter ground. Then Vali faced them and ordered them to stop. The light beam on his head flipped around and hit them. They squinted and shielded their eyes. He laughed. "You're getting like me now. Mole people."

He motioned them to move into a niche in the wall. This was recent work, thought Ethan. The stone was lighter in color. The cut marks were visible. Someone had carved out a narrow slot about six feet high, ending in a blank rock wall. "Come on, boys. Don't be shy."

They moved into the cut. For the first time, Ethan got

really close to Vali. In the confined space, a distinctly unpleasant smell enveloped him. No baths in the underworld, thought Ethan.

"Look here," said Vali as he pointed to a small, circular, machined piece of metal and glass built into the stone wall. "Go ahead. Check it out."

Ethan leaned in and peered into the eyepiece. Bright light hit the back of his eyes; he looked at another world. The fish-eye lens provided a wide-angle view of a tunnel. This wasn't an old mine shaft or a natural cave. This was new, about twenty feet in diameter, with smooth, black, glass-like surfaces except for the floor, which appeared to be concrete. Regularly spaced overhead lights provided shadowless illumination. It looked like some kind of bunker. Then he saw something even more astounding; the headlight of a vehicle approached quickly. A train of vehicles moved from right to left, creating flickering dark and light images. He saw no people, only about fifteen bright-yellow tubular railroad cars with rubber tires and synthetic housings and carriages. They slid in and out of his vision without sound, like a silent movie. When it was gone, he turned and offered Zak a view. While his friend peered into the device, Ethan looked at Vali. "What the hell was that?" he asked, almost talking to himself.

Vali cocked his head. "That, my friend, is the real world. Something you know little about."

For the better part of the next hour, Vali, Zak, and Ethan sat on the floor of the mine shaft talking. Vali was patient and handled their questions in an orderly fashion. Where does the tunnel lead? Who is in charge? What is it for?

Vali obviously enjoyed his role as an educator. "This tunnel is part of a nationwide system of tunnels— storage facilities, living quarters, transportation systems. Black-budget government projects. Right now, hundreds of thousands of people fill underground cities from one coast to the other. Super-secret. The public never knew."

Ethan was puzzled. "But why are people living like this? There's no war. No calamity."

Vali shook his head. "You're right. There never was a threat. The threats were fabrications. First, the Russians. Then undefined 'evildoers.' Then insurgents and revolutionaries. In time, the real government evaporated, leaving only a shell of shills above ground. Normal people were systematically eliminated. They called them 'useless eaters.' Birth-control programs, phony immunization programs, chemtrails, meaningless wars, weather wars, mini-plagues, extermination camps. You name it, they did it. Robots and software replaced people. Work disappeared. The average guy became unnecessary for the people on top. The only people who counted were the unseen special people. Thirteen mucho-money families and their minions who ran the show."

"What about the great cities? They didn't just disappear." Ethan spoke loudly.

"No. I used to live in one. New York. It didn't disappear. But it became a dying hellhole. Nobody would want to live there. God knows what it's like now. I got out of there nine years ago, and it was unbearable then. I lost everyone. I left them all behind. My family. All my friends.

"There are people living above ground. If that's what you want to call it. And your news stories about the dangers of the outside world are true. But the outside world is not what you think. Except for parts of Colorado and the Las Vegas area, there is no real living above ground. It's either a lawless, uncivilized mess or a tightly controlled military facility. Except for cute little research towns like Mystic Heights. For special, lucky people like you. Maybe a couple dozen of those. Most likely, there's some nice vacation spots out there, too. For the elite."

"*What about the other people?*" signed Zak, with Ethan translating.

"The other people are going, going, gone," answered

Vali. "My guess. The population of the country is down to about fifty million. And the way it's going, give it another twenty years, and it will be less than a million."

"Are there many like you?" asked Ethan.

"You mean underground people?"

Ethan nodded.

"There are enough of us to worry the old lady. We survive, we reproduce, we disrupt, and we hope for a better future. That's about it," said Vali.

Vali kept going for a few more minutes, and then, after glancing at his new timepiece, he announced they had to move on. He ducked into another recess out of view and returned with a small black satchel in his hand a few moments later. He told them they had to catch low tide. They traveled on through the mine works, downhill. After another hour of travel, Ethan smelled something familiar and comforting. It was the smell of the sea. Soon, they heard the sound of waves. Finally, they saw a glimmer of light at the end of the tunnel.

"This is it," said Vali. "Can't go any further. It's not safe for me. Look. The water's already come through the entrance. Tide's coming in. Our timing must be off. You've got to get going, or you'll be trapped here."

Ethan turned to face him. "Where do you live? Are there others like you?"

"Time for you to go. Don't try to leave Mystic Heights. You two are 'chosen people.' Forget me and forget what I told you. Play their game. Ain't no other choice. Make yourself useful, and you might be allowed to survive."

Zak's hands flew into a flurry of conversation.

Vali looked at him, shook his head, and offered his hand. They shook hands.

"Oh, yeah. Make a left turn when you get to the water. That's the way to town. If you turn right, you'll only find more water and more rock face. Bad choice." Then Vali handed Ethan the satchel. "Use this if you need to. Thanks for the watch. You better get going. Good luck." He smiled, turned, and jogged into the darkness.

Ethan opened the bag to check its contents and quickly closed it.

"What is it?"

"A pigeon," answered Ethan. "The communications medium of the future.

-Chapter IV-

Against the Tide

They watched Vali run away, the bouncing beam of his headlamp silently tracking his uphill progress.

"We'd better get out of here. At high tide, the entrance will be completely covered with water. Let's go!" said Ethan.

The time travelers jogged down the tunnel. The dim twilight filtering through the rocky opening at the end was the only light source. They encountered a flood of icy seawater about a hundred feet from the entrance. At first, they pussyfooted. After only a few tenuous steps, the tops of their shoes were covered. They looked down as if they were surprised that the water was wet and cold. But Ethan realized there was no recourse. They couldn't go back into the cave; they had to leave now. They slogged ahead, their legs kicking up plumes of water as they struggled against the tide. At the entrance, they stepped out into the flat, gray, cold madness of sea and sky. Directly ahead lay the Atlantic Ocean: bleak, dark, and vast. Ethan glanced to the right, then to the left. To either side, he saw scattered black boulders and churning water. He looked up and realized they were at the bottom of a sheer vertical rock face. The cave opening was but a pinhole in the massive cliff.

Above the noise of wind and crashing waves, Ethan shouted, "This could be Smuggler's Cove, Zak. Vali said to go left. I hope he's right."

No longer protected by the cave and totally exposed to the elements, the two men worked to remain upright in the surging water. Ethan held the bag containing the pigeon high. As the undulating waves soon doused them with icy water, he grabbed Zak with his free hand and pulled him. "We've got to get moving. The tide is rising, it's getting dark, and I'm freezing." Zak didn't argue the point. When a wave receded, the seawater all but disappeared. Seconds later, when another crashed again, they were knee-deep. It was painfully difficult to maintain balance and move ahead. As they walked carefully on a slimy rock bed, each incoming wave shoved them into the wall of rock, then sucked them out. They followed a slow zigzag path, dodging large boulders. Ethan led the way, but in time he found their current route impossible. It was too difficult and too dangerous to deal with the waves. Away from the wall, the water was deeper and colder but calmer. That was his new path. Slowly they progressed, the water up to their thighs, the view ahead offering nothing but black water and fading light.

Zak grabbed Ethan by the shoulder, who turned and almost dropped the bag into the water. Zak signed something, but Ethan didn't have time to notice. He shouted, "We have to move faster, Zak! The tide is moving in quickly." Then Ethan tripped over a submerged rock. He stumbled and fell into the water, turning his body as he went down, holding his arm up and keeping the bird bag dry. In the cold, watery darkness, he stared up at the surface. A shadow appeared. Zak gathered him in; in one swift action, his powerful arms lifted Ethan to a standing position. Ethan was stunned by the experience. But his mind was still functioning. Dripping wet and incredibly cold, he knew he was in trouble now. Unless they found shelter soon, he would not survive the hypothermia.

"Thanks, Zak," he whispered his words, and they were lost to the wind. He held his arm out. "At least the bird...didn't take a bath." He coughed uncontrollably and shivered involuntarily.

Wearing a look of concern, Zak gestured to him to move ahead. They pushed on, slipping and sliding, battered by freezing water and fierce winds. Ethan glanced up at the cliff and saw the rock edge sloped down. Dimly in the distance, he could see the point where the dark mass of this wall of rock merged with the sea. They were making progress, but he was dead tired. He looked back. He caught a glimpse of Zak struggling through the foaming water a few feet behind. He wanted to toss the pigeon into the water. Why keep the stupid thing? But he hung on. Head down and determined to make it, he pushed ahead.

Ten grueling minutes later, at the point of total exhaustion, he sensed a difference in his footing. The surface was flatter. He looked up. The rock face to his left was all but gone. Above its ragged edge, the familiar lights of Randall Tower appeared in the distant sky. They were almost safe. Hardened sand beneath his feet told the tale. They headed toward the frozen, snowy beach. The transfer from water to land required that he and Zak hold hands. They stumbled through the treacherous blend of seawater and ice. Their feet cracked and penetrated the brittle surface, and with each step, the ice grabbed them like the jaws of an animal trap. When Ethan eased his captured foot out of the icy web, he felt the knife-sharp edges cut through his socks into his nearly frozen flesh. Finally, they crossed the barrier. They walked inland. The sea now only rumbled behind them. Their feet crunched atop the snow-packed beach. The wind eased. The maelstrom had ended. It was now just a peaceful winter evening on the New England shore.

He saw a car's headlights traveling on Memorial Drive, heading into town. He turned back to face his friend. Zak, bent over, was moving very slowly. He wanted to smile, but his face wouldn't cooperate. His voice was weak. "We made it, Zak. We're back." He held the bird bag high. "Including this stupid bird." He peered into the bag. The pigeon looked up at him. He cooed and bobbed his head. He seemed unaffected. His black eyes held no emotion—no fear, no exhaustion, no cold.

"*Is he alive?*" asked Zak, his semi-frozen fingers flailing almost incoherently.

Ethan chuckled and shook his head. "Ignorance is bliss. Apparently, he enjoyed the ride. Let's go home."

"You boys are swimming against the tide," said Dr. Currant.

"We were last night, A.C. We almost didn't make it."

"That's not what I'm talking about."

"What do you mean?" asked Ethan. "We cleared the way for Franklin Roosevelt to be elected President of the United States, right? We think something good will come of that."

"Someone has to do something," said Zak. "You two never mentioned the reality of life here in this beautiful 'think tank' called Mystic Heights." Zak was wearing his *Voicenator* now and enjoying the freedom of expression it provided. "This country is really in bad shape. I don't see how intelligent people like you can be so complacent."

"Intelligent people don't hijack my machine and abandon my best friend's only daughter," Currant turned toward Warren Wright and then fixed his gaze back upon Zak and Ethan, "and then get lost in time and space. Worse yet, you could have revealed my machine to MOM."

Ethan rallied to the defense of his friend. "But we did give FDR a chance to change *The History*, right?"

"How would we know? Our world here hasn't changed a bit. You know that. You're the only people who remember that past world. You may have memories of martial law in America in 1932 and the creation of a dictatorship, but we don't. We can only take your word for that. I don't doubt that you are telling the truth. Something motivated you three to time-travel there. But I can tell you that there have been no big historical changes as far as I know."

"FDR became the President of the United States, right?" declared Ethan.

There was a pause of silence. "I'm afraid not, son," said Wright solemnly.

"What do you mean, Dad?"

"Franklin Roosevelt was elected in 1932, but he never took office. He was assassinated on February 15, 1933."

Wright's very private, quiet, secure home office became a tomb for the moment. Ethan threw his head back and looked around the table. Zak gently scratched the back of his head, looking thoroughly confused. Mr. Wright sat with his hands clasped together on the table, eyes lowered. And Dr. Currant sat on the edge of his chair, wild-eyed and smiling triumphantly.

"He's dead?"

"That's right," Currant popped in loudly. "Your impromptu Save America field trip was a giant waste of time. You forget time is like an ocean. And the *TimeTravelle* is only a tiny time-traveling rowboat. One that requires a trained navigator. Our 1963 excursion was fun...nostalgia on steroids. I got to visit my family. I kept my brother out of trouble. I picked up a very cool '55 Chevy. Your old man regained the use of his legs." He nodded with pride. "All good stuff. But in the end, Mr. Kennedy was not resurrected. He had his head blown off in Dallas. And the guys who did it just kept going. The corrupt American Ship of State still plies the waters of time. Maybe now the public is slightly more aware, but they're still clueless. They still believe the propaganda. Anyway, I guided that first trip from start to finish. Not you. And then you kids decided you could do it yourself. Just flip a switch, and off you go in the *TimeTravelle*. It's not that simple. So now your FDR is dead, and your sister is stuck...god knows where...in 1932."

"OK, A.C.," said Warren Wright. "I'm sure Zak and Ethan get your point. Let's not beat it...and them...into the ground. Let's focus on Emma. She exists, but not in our time. That's what's important now. All of you must go back and save her. Forget about FDR. Just bring back my daughter."

-Chapter V-

Currant Confides

The next day Zak and Ethan met Dr. Currant. His hidden underground bunker was buried deep beneath the rocky cliff overlooking Smuggler's Cove. Their flight into the lab had been tightly scheduled by Currant. They were smoothly transported via the *TimeTravelle* from the giant chess board to the landing pad below through thirty feet of granite.

Slightly dazed from their short trip through time and space, they shook off its effects under the bright lights of the lab. Zak heard a nearby voice, which he recognized as Dr. A.C. Currant. "See how smoothly things go under the direction of a pro? This, my friends, is the way it should have been at the end of your little illegal excursion. Come down, sit, and have a cup of coffee."

Zak and Ethan ambled down the ramp and followed Currant into the depths of his lair. The inventor and physicist was a different man today, thought Ethan. He acted as if yesterday's hyperbolic and caustic lecturing had never happened. A.C. looked impressive and commanding, flowing about wearing his crisp white lab coat. Today he was also cordial. He served coffee to his guests as they took seats around the lab table.

Industrial light fixtures hung low, giving this part of the lab a fairly cozy feel compared to the cavernous atmosphere. In this almost intimate setting, Ethan focused on A.C. Currant, who seated himself at the head of the table. He was getting older, his hair now more salt than pepper, but his eyes were still bright, his face clean and handsome, and his back ramrod straight. He was in his late seventies, yet he remained intact physically and mentally. He lifted his coffee mug in a wordless toast, nodded, and drank the fresh brew.

"Well, my young fellow travelers." He smiled his wide, white, captivating smile. "You look rested and ready for action. Welcome again to the Wonderful World of Dr. Currant." He laughed, and Ethan and Zak presented half-hearted smiles. "Let's talk. Your father's not here. It's just us. We can get right down to business. I do want to apologize for my abruptness at yesterday's meeting with Warren. I should have taken into account your condition. After all, you had a very weird return flight."

Ethan was puzzled by the contriteness of Currant's approach. "We did have a rough landing. Maybe you can explain what we did wrong." He was fishing.

Currant smiled and tossed the bait back. "What do you think was wrong with your approach, other than its unauthorized use of my machine?"

"Our take-off markers were unclear. Ill-defined. Almost unrecognizable. The top of this hill is quite a bit different in the year 1932."

"I'll bet."

"There's no war memorial. No designated positions. No definition. We had the timing all right, but we couldn't be sure about our locations. And Emma wasn't with us. Does that make a difference?"

Currant sipped his coffee, set the cup down gently, and looked directly at Ethan. He smiled. "You'll never know. I'm not about to educate you on the workings of my machine. I will mention temporal markers. Something you wouldn't understand. But that's all you'll get. Don't ever try that again. You were lucky that you made it back to *this* time. It was just as possible that you could have returned to the old reality. The one in which FDR remained an unknown, drunken dilettante architect. In that case, your sister Emma might have been lost in time, along with your memories. So be it. You're here now. Thanks to you, we know she is in Washington, D.C., in the year 1933. Right?"

"She should be," said Ethan. "We left her in the hands of a man who works for Roosevelt. Jack Travers."

"In the hands of Jack Travers...," said Currant slowly

and deliberately. "I'll bet. A little love affair too, eh?" Currant smiled.

"He seemed to genuinely care for her," said Zak.

"That's great," said Currant. "Let's hope they didn't decide to take off for South America. So, tell me everything about your travels. Every detail, no matter how seemingly insignificant. Everything."

For the next hour, Zak and Ethan related the events of their time-travel excursion intended to rescue Franklin Delano Roosevelt's political career. Dr. Currant listened intently, interrupted often, and took notes.

"And you say this guy, Jack Travers, was working for FDR?"

"Actually, he may have been working for Mrs. Roosevelt, but the net effect is the same. He was an advance man and a troubleshooter for the FDR campaign," replied Zak.

"And you happened upon him at a Bonus Marcher rally? He just showed up in the crowd?"

"We think he was sent there by Mrs. Roosevelt as a scout. It was a big day with General Butler speaking and tensions running high."

"Did he approach you?"

Zak and Ethan looked at each other. Ethan shrugged his shoulders. "I think he was interested in Emma. She was the big attraction."

"Right. Do you trust him?"

"Travers?"

"Can you confide in him? Would he help us?"

Zak smiled. "Well, he got us out of the hands of the FBI. I thought we were toast. Yeah. He was very helpful. And he watched over Emma like a mother hen."

"Good. Jack Travers gives us a necessary toehold in time. Don't worry. We'll find little Emma."

Apparently, having heard enough, Currant slid off his stool, stood, and took a few steps back. He stretched his entire body. "I'm getting old, boys. I'm seventy-seven now. Everything starts to tighten up. But I shouldn't complain." He returned, sat down, and rested his forearms on the table, his hands linked together. The bright overhead light reflected off his face, revealing the onset of lines and wrinkles. Currant was beginning to show his age.

"You heard that my brother Patrick died?" said Currant.

They said nothing but nodded.

"He did. While you were gone, I'm sorry to say. At least he went quickly. You know, he wasn't much older than me, but he was out of sync with medical advancements. He was born a few years too early. Just missed that boat. And I'll miss him. But needless to say, our JFK trip gave him a new life. And I'm grateful to you for acquiescing to my personal needs. He was a great man."

Some uncomfortable silence followed. Currant himself broke the spell. "Anyway, Patrick's passing got me thinking. As you know, I really wasn't on board with your crusade to save the world then. And I was burned up with your latest venture." He paused, took a deep breath, looked up at the ceiling, and then lowered his head, gazing at Ethan and Zak. He nodded gently as he spoke. "But I realize now that I...uh...I only have a few more decades. Or just a few more years. Who knows? Maybe I'm getting religion, but I've come to the realization that exhuming this FDR guy may not be such a bad idea."

"What are you saying, A.C.? I thought our only focus was to get Emma back safely," said Ethan.

"Well, maybe not the only focus," said Currant. "We're only going back to 1933 this one time. Why can't we retrieve her and save FDR? She would want that. And who knows, maybe I can make this world just a little bit better before I leave it. It could use some improvement."

"So you want to do it? You want to save FDR? Are we going to tell Dad? He's totally against that. He just wants Emma back. He made that quite clear."

Currant snorted. "Hell no! He'll never buy it. Keep this between us, boys."

Ethan and Zak were wide-eyed in wonderment now.

"*Hijole!*" exclaimed Zak. "Now we're talking."

The inventor stood. "Of course, I'll be in charge of this flight?"

Zak and Ethan looked at each other, then back to Currant. They nodded in submission. Currant seemed pleased with himself. He spoke quietly, almost as if talking to himself or his dead brother. "I'm looking forward to living in the 1930s. More respect for older folk in those days. I think I'll cut quite a figure." He pulled away from the table, straightened up, put his hand to his chin, and looked at Zak and Ethan. "You ever see those old black-and-white photos of the JFK assassination? You know. Right when it's all coming apart. I was there, right in the middle of one of the most important moments in American history. I'm the fellow pumping the black umbrella up and down. Now, they call me the 'Umbrella Man." He chuckled. "I'm looking forward to more of that action. Today's world just doesn't cut it anymore."

Ethan sensed Currant's angst. Mystic Heights was, after all, a cocoon for those living there: lovely, warm, and cozy. But dark place. The townspeople were blind to the reality of their world. They performed their daily chores for the system, unaware that society had imploded into a tidy computerized, robotized world run by a few very rich, compulsive control freaks. Currant must know that at any moment, Mystic Heights could become obsolete. For all its usefulness now, as a breeding place for men and women to plug into the research and development community, it could disappear overnight, like many other unnecessary towns and cities. The creators of *The History*, the ultimate rulers, had found ways to evolve a world without the "useless eaters." That was their word for everyone other than themselves. They were the chosen, and all the other people were significantly less important than cows or chickens.

Ethan could only speculate about A.C. Currant and

his sudden conversion to their cause. But Currant could operate the *TimeTravelle*; and without that nothing could happen. Emma could not return, FDR would remain dead, and the world would continue to self-destruct.

LOG of Zak Newman
December 28, 2032 (local time): 11:22

So we wait for our return trip to begin. According to Dr. Currant, we will leave for 1933 in a few days. It's good that Mr. Wright and Jacques Dufour created a cover story for our absence from Cordwell University last semester. That tale was about the three of us assisting Mr. Wright in researching and writing a book titled Great Investigators of the 19th Century. Of course, Emma, Ethan, and I are continuing to work on this fictitious tome this semester. Therefore we will again not attend school. Since Mr. Wright is actually working on this book, there will be a final product to buttress this ruse. So far, as far as we know, MOM is buying this B.S. We can hope.

A.C. has been gone for about a week. He said he was off to do some "pre-tuning," as he calls it. According to him, Ethan and I have already been introduced to the 1930s culture with our trip to the Bonus March camp. But, unlike our previous venture with the good doctor, he wasn't alive in 1933. He doesn't really have a good feel for the times. He says he's created a very strong backstory for himself as Emma and Ethan's uncle. That should be a laugh.

He has asked us a million questions about our flight to 1932, but he wants a real taste. So last week, he left in the TimeTravelle to visit the world of 1933. He's going to Mystic Heights, Boston, and who knows where else? Before he left, he told us he would be preparing the groundwork for all of us—clothes, money, identification samples, purchasing train tickets and accessories. And "veritas." This is his name for the little things that give us credibility, such as pocket knives, old photos, match packs, pens, books, etc. I suspect that he will not carry any of these items back and forth in time other than possibly the money he will have gathered. It's his intention to, in his words, "farm the past" by using his foreknowledge of events to make 1933 money. I'm interested to find out how he does this.

Ethan and I were quite upset when we were told about Mr. Roosevelt's death. The future DID change after our first flight to 1932. Martial law for the entire country was not initiated. President Herbert Hoover left office; the 1932 election was not canceled. And FDR lived long enough to be elected, but he never made it to his inauguration. Sadly, on February 15, 1933, in Miami, he died from bullet wounds inflicted by another "lone nut" assassin, Giuseppe Zangara. This sounds like the JFK assassination in Dallas 30 years later—another crazy guy who decides to take out the president. According to the new version of The History, this little Italian immigrant was upset because he had stomach pains and he didn't like authority (really, who does?). Surprisingly, they didn't say he was a "communist," the quintessential bogeyman name in the '30s. And he wasn't a three-name monster like most other American assassins. According to newspapers printed the next day, Zangara said: "I have done my own thinking, and I have reached this decision myself." Wow, that takes the edge off a conspiracy. Very convenient. In short order, he was tried and convicted of murder and put to death in the electric chair little more than a month later, on March 20, 1933.

There was no Jack "Sparky" Ruby-type in this one to silence the assassin, just swift, and I mean very swift justice. Zangara apparently was a strange little man. His last words were: "Viva, the poor people. Viva The Camorra! Push the button, go and push the button." Then they threw the switch on the other "Sparky" and shot a couple thousand volts into his tiny body. And that was the end of him and any discussion of the crime. With his words—"The Camorra"—he may as well have said, "I work for the Mafia."

FDR was dead. His assassin was dead. And the new

Vice President, John Nance Garner, the former speaker of the House of Representatives and a native Texan, was sworn in as the 32nd President of the United States. They called him "Cactus Jack." Ah, these colorful monikers fill 20th-century history.

Onto the past. Hopefully, we will find Emma, fix FDR's presidency, and slide back into a 2033 that is a better place to live.

P.S. Ethan gave the pigeon to Jacques Dufour for safekeeping. He named him "Marconi." Dufour seemed pleased to have a new companion.

End 12-28-2032

-Chapter VI-

Chicago 1933

Chicago was now a hundred years old. 1932 was almost gone, and 1933, the year of Chicago's anticipated redemption, would arrive in a few hours. The Depression continued to weigh hard on the citizens of the second-largest city in the country. Banks failed, city services suffered, and taxes went uncollected. Joblessness was pervasive. In the fading light of this last day of 1932, the people hoped lawlessness and corruption would drift into the past. The new year and the coming World's Fair promised a new beginning for millions of Chicagoans. Of course, Jack Travers knew the fair also provided incredible profits for those in control. As always, Chicago was "the city on the make."

He was on assignment from Eleanor Roosevelt. There was a possibility that she and her husband might participate in the upcoming May opening of the Century of Progress exposition or at least in the festivities sometime during its run. Today, Jack Travers was acting as an advance-man. It was his job to verify the lay of the land. That view of the local landscape would include his assessment of the politicians, specifically the relatively new mayor of Chicago, Anton Cermak. He would also provide a status report on the Mob. Mrs. Roosevelt was not so concerned about threats to their lives. She wanted to avoid the embarrassment of the Roosevelts sharing the national spotlight with another batch of murdered mobsters. With over seven hundred gangland murders since 1920, Chicago had achieved national recognition for its violence, corruption, and mayhem. Al Capone, who at this moment was serving an eleven-year sentence for income tax evasion, was famous worldwide. His Chicago was known as the "murder capital" of the

United States.

But Prohibition was about to end, and the people were looking forward to drinking a legal glass of beer and toasting the demise of mobster activity when the booze cash cow was slaughtered. Of course, Jack knew that the "Outfit," as Capone's gang was called, would not pull up stakes. They would just explore other areas to impose their influence: gambling, vice, and labor control. And the gang wars would continue. The 1929 St. Valentine's Day Massacre didn't end the competition for the dirty dollar. Like Roger Touhy's northwest suburban crew, other gangland figures continued to battle the Outfit for control.

And, of course, the new mayor had to be considered. Mayor Cermak wanted to crush the Outfit. Without mentioning his own agenda, Cermak promised the citizens of Chicago that he would get rid of the mobsters. To those in the know, Cermak's nickname was "Ten Percent Tony." By taking his cut from the awards of public projects and licensing and allowing thieves to profit as he looked the other way, this self-made politician, this man of the people, became a millionaire several times over, making a mockery of his modest annual salary. For Anton Cermak, the former coal miner and now machine-politician kingpin, this night, December 31, 1932, New Year's Eve, was to mark the sunset of the old Outfit regime and the dawn of a new day, a new year, and a new Chicago syndicate to permanently replace Capone's empire.

The transition had apparently begun just a few days ago. Travers had read the sensational stories in the local newspapers, but he wanted to know the details. That was his job. He invited the key crime reporters from the top three Chicago dailies, the *Chicago Tribune*, the *Chicago Daily News*, and the *Chicago American*, to celebrate the New Year with a night on the town. The first stop was the famous Green Mill, a North Side Capone speakeasy. After an hour of partying, everyone got sufficiently "wet." They left that joint and braved the icy ten-degree temperature and the wind blowing in from Lake Michigan. As they walked, the raucous voices of the seven jolly people bounced off the walls of the brick buildings that lined Lawrence Avenue. New Year's Eve had begun. A few minutes of controlled stumbling brought them to the Aragon Ballroom.

The party continued once settled inside the colonnaded and romantic Moorish dance barn. Travers gazed at the shifting mass of couples on the dance floor and then turned to focus on his table of guests. Johnny Thomas, Sid Metz, and Lou "The Nose" Campia nestled between the babes: a blonde, a brunette, and a redhead. What else could they ask for? They laughed at a joke Sid had told about a farmer's daughter. Jack laughed too. Wayne King's orchestra finished their set just as the laughter died down. It was a good time to extract some information. "So what about that Nitti thing?" asked Jack loudly. "You boys must have the real scoop. What's going on there?"

Sid, a short man, wearing wire-framed glasses and sporting thinning, slicked-back black hair, jumped on it. He extended his right hand, made a finger gun, and pointed it at the blonde across the table. "Bang, bang, bang. Nitti went down. They finally got him."

She laughed loudly and pretended to be hit. "Don't shoot me honey...yet," she said with a lilt and a smile that hinted broadly that more than just corks would be popping at midnight.

"Ain't she a pip?" Sid's eyebrows rose in delight.

Ignoring the wordplay, Travers continued his questioning. "Who's *they*?"

"That's the '$64 question'," replied Lou. "It's really difficult to sort out the players in this town, Jack. Probably something like Washington."

Travers looked at him and wondered why they called him "The Nose." They should have called him "The Ears," he thought. He had ears like Alfalfa from the *Our Gang* comedies. "Democrats and Republicans," said Travers flatly. "Some honest, some not. Backed up by thousands of bureaucrats." He saw Johnny Thomas leaning into the redhead's ear and whispering. She smiled and faintly blushed. "Johnny. What about it? The papers said that Nitti shot a cop, and the cop shot back."

Johnny, the looker of the trio, pulled his nose out of the redhead's hair. "I'll be back, sweetheart," he mumbled quietly. He faced Travers. "I think the whole thing was a setup from the get-go. This cop, Henry Lang. We know him. He and his buddy Miller are part of the mayor's handpicked team. We call it the 'hoodlum squad' in the papers. They busted into Nitti's office over on LaSalle and Wacker. They were just there to cause trouble. That's all. And they did."

Metz chimed in. "Face it, Jack, Chicago's full of trouble. Mobsters are getting killed at the rate of one a day. Most of them worked for Capone. Cermak got elected, and he's cleanin' house. He cut out Mayor Thompson's people. It's Tony's town now. And he's out to get Al Capone's people. The mayor's an uneducated brute, but he's a damn good organizer. He's got people jumpin'. The police force is his personal army. Every day they're fightin' battles with Nitti's gang. He's been raidin' their hideouts and puttin' their henchmen in jail. Nitti was just the big fish. Cermak's out to hook all of them. Bring them in. Cut off their heads. And dump them in the trash." The women responded to this conversation by making faces. "Sorry, ladies. Just a figure of speech."

"At the end of his term, when Big Bill Thompson was hanging onto the fifth floor of city hall, he lost control of the mob. Cermak's just trying to get back to the status quo," said Lou. "At the *American*, we see Cermak as a reformer...not a savior."

"So he's not a bohunk version of Jesus Christ, Lou?"

"To the bohunks, he is. As far as they're concerned, he's a miracle worker."

Jack pulled out a pack of Luckies from his shirt pocket. It was his habit now. His work this past year on Roosevelt's campaign trail had been arduous, and as much as he hated the idea of addiction, he now craved both the nicotine and the ritual of smoking. He tapped a cigarette on the back of his hand to pack it and then lit it with a silver lighter that featured an engraved insignia on its face. Casually, he blew out a lungful of smoke toward the ceiling, and the cloud mixed with the smoky discharges of hundreds of others, creating a permanent gray haze that floated above like a coal town winter sky. Colored spotlights, reflecting off the rotating mirrored ball hanging overhead, rhythmically pierced the cloud of smoke. The visual effect was hypnotic. Emma, the woman he loved, was on his mind. Travers drifted for a moment staring at the smoke as if seeking an answer from the muse. It was brief but long enough to shuffle the conversational cards. Wayne King and his orchestra returned. His reporter friends and the women cracked open another subject, and the music began again— "Dream a Little Dream of Me." Jack wanted to resume his inquiry into local politics, but the opportunity had passed.

"So, Mr. Jack Travers. Do you dance?" asked the brunette who sat between him and the *Daily News* reporter.

He looked at the woman. She was a few years younger than he was, mid-twenties maybe. But she looked older. The Depression could do that. She was attractive, confident, and savvy in her sparkling, clingy, V-neck yellow dress looking like a flirtatious canary.

She caught his eyes, sizing her up. "Like what you see, Jack?"

He smiled. "You are one pretty girl, Anne."

"I'm impressed," she said. "You remembered my name, and I like the 'girl' part."

"I never forget a name. Especially when it's attached to a pretty face."

She pouted in a sexy, knowing manner as if Jack had somehow reopened a long-closed door in her mind. "Dance?" she asked.

He snuffed out his cigarette, stood, and reached for

her hand. The band played as the new couple found a spot on the crowded floor. The air was hot, without much room to move. The dance was simply a way for men and women to cuddle vertically. Jack held her loosely as they danced, but she purposefully brought her body close. She's been around the block a few times, he thought. And he couldn't help becoming aroused, and she couldn't help but notice.

"I think you like me, Jack." She laughed lightly. "Did you know you have the most beautiful brown eyes?"

"I can't see my eyes."

"And your 'stache...I just love it." She gently rubbed her fingers over Jack's pencil mustache and giggled. "Did anyone ever say you look like Gilbert Roland?"

"I've been called lots of things, but not that. I like his movies, though."

"Must be the tall, dark, and handsome part. I think I'll pretend I'm dancing with him right now." She laughed lightly and snuggled closer. She whispered, "You're a good dancer, Jack. I'll bet you're good at everything." He felt her warm breath on his neck, and her lips brushed against his earlobe. They waltzed about slowly. She pulled her head off his shoulder and looked into his eyes. "So how come a good-looking fellow like you is all alone on New Year's Eve?"

"I'm on business."

"I can tell," she said while purposely pressing her pelvis into his.

"You should be keeping my newspaper boys happy, Anne," he said, deflating her balloon. "I'm off the market."

She pulled away quickly. "I should have known. All the good ones are taken. That's the story of my life."

"Sorry, but I have to admit, you make it interesting."

She frowned. The song ended. They separated, applauded lightly, and returned to the table. It appeared as though the others had decided it was time to do something else. They were all standing now.

"Let's go back to the Green Mill, Jack," said Johnny

Thomas. "We need to gas up again. This place is getting stale."

"Wanna take the secret tunnel, girls?" taunted Metz.

They giggled. "That sounds like fun." said the redhead.

"They say there's an underground tunnel between here and the Mill. You drop down right under the bar. You know about that, Jack?"

Jack shook his head.

"They only use that when the cops spring a raid," said Johnny Thomas. "And the boys always get advance notice."

"Your call," said Jack. "It's your night, guys."

They walked back to the Green Mill nightspot and luckily found a booth. It was a tight fit. The boys and the girls had paired up now, with Jack as the "chaperone." He knew Sid Metz was married, but that wasn't slowing him down tonight. Metz squeezed Anne like he owned her, and she slid closer to him. He had told Jack that his wife was visiting relatives in Des Moines for the holidays and that he had every intention of enjoying the evening. The other two men were single. Human nature floated on an unending river of booze, following a serpentine path to the sea of love. Everyone and everything grew louder as the evening progressed. The musicians played with tribal intensity. Somebody yelled that it was midnight in New York, and everyone broke into celebration and hugs and kisses. After another round of drinks, there was a toast to the death of Prohibition.

"It's only a matter of time now," said Sid Metz. "They just missed the vote to repeal. But Roosevelt will take care of it when he gets in." Metz looked around. "Hey, I got a story for you. You know, Joe E. Lewis used to perform here. But one day, he decided to take his talent across the street."

"Bad idea," interrupted Johnny.

"Lemme finish," demanded Metz. "This is my story."

He downed his whiskey. "You remember Lewis." He mimed smoking a cigar and, in an imitation of Joe E. Lewis' voice, said: "'Behind every great woman is a great behind.' Funny guy. Anyway, so Lewis does this. He opens his act down the street at another joint. Well, Jack McGurn..." He lowered his voice and looked around for a second. "Machine Gun Jack McGurn and his boys took care of him. McGurn has a piece of this place, so he had reason to be upset. Three guys...nobody knows who for sure...entered Lewis' hotel room and remodeled his face and tongue with a butcher knife. Lewis almost died. So don't make any wise guy comments in this joint, gals. This is the real thing," he said, his voice returning to normal.

"Speaking of unbridled violence. What about Nitti? Is he going to make it?" asked Jack.

"I hear he's making a comeback, believe it or not," said Lou. "They moved him to Jefferson Park Hospital. His father-in-law's a doctor. Doctor Ronga. He's taking care of him now. I think he's going to make it."

"So Cermak's guys raided the office, Nitti pulled a gun, and they shot him?"

"That's the official story," said Lou, "but Ronga says Nitti never pulled a gun. Nitti stuffed a piece of paper in his mouth when they came to arrest him, and when they tried to extract it, the gun battle ensued. Nitti was hit three times. Harry Lang plugged him in his neck, chest, and gut. Lang says Nitti fired at him, and he does have a gunshot wound in his left arm."

"What's the unofficial story?" asked Travers.

The three newsmen looked at each other until finally, Johnny Thomas spoke. "Who knows? You can't believe any of these cops or crooks." He paused. "But, I'd put my money on Frank Nitti. He's a smart cookie. He's 'the man' now that Big Al is in the big house. I would say it was a bad idea to try to frame him. But first, he has to live. We'll see."

"What about the note that he ate?" asked Travers.

Metz caught this one. "The lab boys are looking at it.

Or so they say. But it probably looks like yesterday's mashed potatoes now."

"What do you think it said? Any idea?"

They all shrugged their shoulders. "Maybe it was a reminder to kill Roger Touhy."

Everyone laughed.

"Is he for real?"

"Who? Touhy?"

"Yes."

"The mayor thinks so," said Lou, "but forget I said that."

Travers only stayed for another fifteen minutes. Then he thanked the boys for joining him, blew a kiss to the women, and moved on, not wanting to be around for the big event. After paying the bill with enough grease to cover two more hours of drinking, he left.

Outside on the sidewalk, the freezing night air caught him by surprise. For a moment, he thought about getting a cab. It was close to the magic hour, with many empty hacks flitting about. But he decided he could use a breather. A walk would do him good. He was only a few blocks from the Edgewater Beach Hotel, where a warm bed awaited. Light snow flurries flew in from across the ice-encrusted beach and danced in the light of the street lamps. The crisp night air was filled with the sound of distant rattlers, car horns, fireworks, and gunshots. The city was excited. Another year of the Great Depression had passed away. The New Year meant little to Jack Travers. To him, the passage of time was just an illusion, a way of keeping score and remembering the sequence of events. But, as he walked alone along this lonely strip of Sheridan Road, his thoughts turned to Emma. He wished he could be with her now to celebrate. She made every day special for him. She was the one person he could count on. The one constant in his life. He turned up the collar of his trench coat and walked faster. "Happy New Year," he mumbled to himself. It was time to come in from the cold.

-Chapter VII-

Tracking Emma

The last time Ethan and Zak rode a train along the East Coast, they bounced around on the wooden floors of boxcars, grubbed food in hobo Jungle towns, and dressed like bums. This time, wearing freshly pressed suits, white shirts, and ties, they rode in style and ate quality meals in the posh dining car. They looked and acted like successful businessmen. On his recent trip back in time, the one he called 'pre-tuning,' A.C. Currant ordered complete outfits for Zak and Ethan from a shop in Mystic Heights. They retrieved their new clothes shortly after time-traveling to Mystic Heights circa 1933. Now, aboard the Pennsylvania Railroad train, The Senator, they moved closer to their destination. The crack train was fast, reliable, and luxurious, compressing the long journey between Boston and Washington, D.C., to less than 10 hours. Powered by a massive, churning steam locomotive, it dragged a smoky ribbon along the snow-covered northern shore of Long Island Sound. Ethan stared out the window at the world of February 1933. The last rays of the sun filtered through the mass of barren trees that undulated across rolling hills. The locomotive's misty steam cloud drifted above the train, hypnotically pulsing the waning sunlight that bounced off the copper-clad roofs of church steeples in the distance. Ethan squinted as brightly reflected sunbeams shot across the countryside into his eyes. He turned back to face Dr. Currant and Zak.

They sat comfortably on coach seats opposite him. Zak was engrossed in a book about Houdini. And Currant, now sporting a Florida tan acquired on his earlier groundbreaking visit to 1933, focused his piercing dark brown eyes on Ethan. Quickly Ethan unlocked his gaze from Currant and looked out the window. Engine soot and steam wafted down, momentarily clouding the view. The rhythmic click-clack of the train's wheels numbed Ethan's mind. He mused about train travel and the passage of time. Currant's backward view of the world outside the train reflected the regular course of time. Everything that happened outside the window—people, towns, rivers, and lakes— rushed past and receded into nothingness.

Ethan thought about the last time he saw Emma. She was in a wheelchair on the balcony of St. Elizabeth's Hospital in Washington, recovering from a battle with tuberculosis. Somehow she survived. He and Zak kissed her goodbye in a time one hundred years past. Then, like the scenery out of the window, time rocketed ahead. He and Zak returned to the future. His remembrance of that time with Emma was small and dim. Time had passed quickly, and now it seemed like a bad dream. He had been responsible for her. He convinced her to travel to 1932 to save Franklin Roosevelt's career. He left her in a boxcar where she was attacked and almost raped by a railroad cop. He brought her to the mud-soaked, danger-filled camp where she met Jack Travers. And he dropped her into the arms of Travers and abandoned her to the care of this stranger. Five months and a hundred years had shot ahead, leaving him and Emma lost in time. He didn't know where she could be found. He hoped she was still in Washington, D.C. But really, he had no way of knowing. The pain of losing his twin sister was intense. It was as if he had lost a part of himself.

"Ethan, what's buzzing around your head?" asked Currant. "You look a little spacey."

"Just thinking about Emma."

"Don't worry. We'll straighten that out. Doc Currant is on the job now."

Zak created a blast of sign language. Ethan began to translate, but Currant interrupted him. "You forget," he bragged, "this old dog has learned a new trick. I can almost understand Mr. Newman. And the answer, Zak, is that I went south on a little journey to Miami. Sun and fun. I wanted to get the lay of the land. You know. Where 'Mr. Z' did his nasty thing."

"Are you talking about Zak?"

Currant laughed. "Not that, 'Mr. Z'. You know. The other 'Mr. Z'. Our guy in Miami.

Zak rolled his eyes, and Ethan nodded and smiled.

A.C. Currant looked around to see if anyone else in the car was listening. Satisfied that their conversation was not being monitored, he continued. "You asked how I got our spending money for this trip." He smiled. "Well, I played the horses at Hialeah Park. And I played them well. I had plenty of winners. Really could pick 'em." He winked. "If you catch my drift."

Ethan assumed the physicist had researched all the horses that finished in the money before leaving on an earlier 1933 flight "Any issues?" asked Ethan.

Currant shook his head. "Not a one. I was very discriminating. Very discreet. He cleared his throat and glanced up the aisle at the rows of businessmen talking, laughing, napping, or reading. Again he sensed no interest. "You won't believe this, but I think I might have seen our friend 'Mr. Z' at the track. He was on the rail. A good-looking, dark-haired young woman was hanging on his arm. I know it was him from the photos I've seen. He's got a distinctive look." Then a middle-aged man walking down the aisle approached them. Currant spotted him and stopped his travelogue. "I'll bring you up to date when we get to our hotel in D.C." He pulled out one of his *veritas* items from his inside pocket, a new deck of playing cards that featured the heads of two racehorses on a plain red background. "How about some cards to pass the time?"

After traveling a century across time and many miles overland, they checked into the Mayflower Hotel and enjoyed a pleasant night's sleep. They ate a light breakfast in the hotel's coffee shop the following day, seated at a window table facing Connecticut Avenue. Currant seemed fascinated by the cavalcade of antique autos cruising the street while Ethan raved over the great prices, seven dollars a night for a double. And Zak appeared to be most interested in the young women passing by on their way to work in government offices. Over coffee, they plotted their plan of attack.

It was decided that Ethan and Zak would visit St. Elizabeth's Hospital, where they last left Emma. Given that the hospital staff might remember them from their visits six months earlier, they hoped to get an address that would lead them to Emma. While they checked out the hospital, Currant said he planned to get the feel of the town. Ethan sensed the old man was totally into the Thirties era. Like a child on his first visit to an amusement park, Currant was actively absorbing the climate and culture of Washington, D.C., 1933. While Ethan and Zak took a cab to the hospital, he intended to spend the day touring the town, checking out the landmarks, and visiting the halls of Congress. Compared to their first time-travel adventure with him in 1963, he seemed genuinely concerned about changing world history and saving the President-elect. This was a welcome change because they all needed to be on the same page to beat the odds and change the history books.

Ethan remembered their first trip as the taxi made its way through the wooded winding road leading to the hilltop hospital that overlooked the city. Emma was deathly sick then. With her brother on one side and Zak on the other, she sat in the cab's back seat, coughing and struggling to breathe. On arrival, the doctors informed them Emma had tuberculosis but could recover in six to eight months. Unsaid was the possibility that she would never recover and she would die.

The cab parked in front of the hospital entrance.

Ethan told the driver to wait. They entered the tuberculosis building and introduced themselves at the reception desk. Ethan explained that they were seeking an address for their sister, who had been a TB patient the previous year. The head nurse was called. While they waited, Zak and the young blonde receptionist exchanged smiles. She attempted to strike up a conversation with some small talk. Although interested, Zak could only respond with open palms and a smile. Ethan informed her that he could hear and understand everything but was mute. She looked saddened and whispered to Zak that she was sorry. Ethan felt for his friend. Unlike Ethan, Zak did quite well with the opposite sex when he could use his *Voicenator*. He was actually quite the ladies' man. But that handy tool, which could not only replace his damaged vocal cords but also automatically translate into different languages, remained dumb and inaccessible in a dresser drawer back in the year 2033. Ethan had often witnessed Zak using French to melt a young woman's heart. But for this trip, he could only rely on his good looks and hope for a date with a girl who could read lips or sign language or just didn't care.

The head nurse arrived. Mid-thirties and dressed in a crisp white uniform, her cap bore a black and gold stripe. She was all business and sized up the situation quickly. She remembered the case. The tall, dark-haired, good-looking female patient and her close friend Mr. Travers. Travers seemed to make a strong impression on her. She even recalled that he was part of the inner circle of Franklin Roosevelt's staff, and she mentioned that he was very caring for Emma.

To Ethan, her tone of voice revealed that she would have preferred to have Jack Travers taking care of her. Ethan wasn't surprised since Travers was handsome, cultivated, and charming. The nurse remembered Ethan because of his height and Zak because he couldn't talk. So much for their charm, thought Ethan. In time, she revealed that Emma made a remarkable recovery and was clear of the disease. She was released about a month after her arrival. The woman directed the receptionist to provide Ethan with Emma's contact information.

Then she spun around with military precision and headed back into the ward area. Dutifully, the young receptionist handwrote the information on an index card and handed it to Ethan. The address didn't mean much to him. It was in town, but he was not familiar enough with the city's neighborhoods to know precisely where she lived. And he couldn't be sure she lived at that address. It was just her last known address. Then the phone jangled on the blonde's desk. She smiled and waved a quick goodbye to Zak as they returned to their waiting taxi.

Chapter VIII

Reunited

It was late afternoon when they returned to the Mayflower. They found Dr. Currant sitting in the main lobby reading a newspaper. After a quick conversation bringing him up to date, they agreed they should visit the address as soon as possible. As Dr. Currant loved to remind everyone, time was of the essence.

They took a cab across town to the address written on the paper. Zak recognized the area. They passed Folger Park and realized they were in the same neighborhood they had lived in for a few weeks in the summer of 1932. It was also within walking distance of Jack Travers' apartment. The cab jerked to a stop in front of a three-story apartment building that faced the park. While Currant paid the driver, Ethan and Zak hunted for the exact address in the half-block-long building. Currant caught up to them.

"Is this it?" he asked.

"Right," said Ethan. "This one. Third floor." They made their way up the red brick steps and entered the building foyer. Ethan scanned the mailboxes. "E. Callan-Wright," he mumbled. "We found her!" He pressed the buzzer button and waited. In the distance, they heard its announcement somewhere inside and above them. Nothing, then he buzzed again.

While they waited, a matronly woman wearing a painted face and carrying a bag of groceries entered the foyer. She wiggled past the men, stopping in front of the second door but hesitating to unlock it. Key in hand, she gave them a fish-eye look. "Can I help you, gentlemen?"

Currant smiled and removed his fedora. "Well, young lady, we are looking for another resident...my niece, Emma. Can you be of any assistance?"

The woman seemed pleased with Currant's courtesy. She returned the smile. "Emma. Your niece. Yes, I know her. She'll be coming home soon...from work. Why don't you all just sit on the front porch and wait?"

Currant thanked her. She waited for them to leave the foyer before opening the door to the stairwell. Ethan and Currant sat down on the brick steps while Zak leaned against the stair railing. "Coming back from work?" asked Ethan.

"Looks like she's settled into her new life pretty well," said Currant. "Let's wait."

Darkness crept over the small public park that lay before them. Along the curb, the lamplighter made his nightly appearance and danced from pole to pole, igniting the flames of the gaslights. Soon it was night. Aside from the distant street lighting, the only illumination came from a small incandescent coach light above the door of the building. The cold was settling into their bones, and they were getting restless.

Zak stood at the base of the stairs and signed, "*I don't think we can wait all night. I'm freezing.*"

"I give it fifteen more minutes, Ethan. These old bones are locking up," said Currant as he momentarily lifted his butt off the cold pavers.

Ethan got up and looked up and down the street. He checked the new wristwatch that Currant had provided him. The green glow of the radium dial read 5:46. Just then, he saw someone on the sidewalk approaching. He rushed down the stairs and ran toward the moving form. The woman, possibly frightened by the onrush, stopped dead in her tracks. Ethan halted a few feet short of her. She lifted the brim of her slouch hat, and the light from the gaslamps exposed her beautiful face. They reached for each other. Sister reunited with brother.

They held the hug for many seconds. Releasing the embrace, Ethan looked at Emma. Her translucent green eyes glazed over, and tears rolled down her cheeks. She smiled bravely. Caught up in the emotion of the moment, she didn't speak. Ethan was elated. She was alive, and he had found her. "Emma. My big sister." He laughed.

"Fifteen minutes older and centuries wiser," she said. She gave Ethan a playful shove. "What took you so long?"

The twins walked hand in hand. Zak and Dr. Currant greeted Emma warmly. Zak gave her a big kiss, and Currant settled for a hug. They were all excited as they followed her up two flights of narrow stairs to her apartment.

Zak smiled and signed as he entered the room and endorsed the tidy one-bedroom unit. "*Not a bad little hideout, Emma.*" He had taken a quick tour around the apartment while the others chitchatted in the living room. Currant and Ethan sat on the sofa, Emma in a wingback chair. The fringed shade on the small, dimly lit table lamp in the front window cast warm light and soft shadows. It was a cozy setting, completed by the comforting crackle and warmth of the compact fireplace and a bottle of brandy that Emma had opened to celebrate the occasion. Zak stirred the fire with a poker and then sat on the sofa arm.

"I do like it," replied Emma. "Jack helped me find it."

"You and Jack?" Ethan stumbled.

"Yes," she said.

"Yes, what?" asked Ethan, regaining his voice.

"We're still together. In fact, we're...engaged." She held up the back of her left hand and exposed a simple silver ring.

Ethan leaned back into the sofa and threw his hands into the air to defend himself from the news. "What?"

"Well, that's something," said A.C. Currant. "Soon, you'll tell us you're expecting a baby?"

Emma frowned. "Back off, fellows. I've been on my own for the past six months. I really had no idea when or if you would return. I decided I'd better make the best of it. So I have. And this thing..." she exposed the ring again on the back of her clenched hand.

"This is required, mandatory, and expedient in 1933

America. You wouldn't want your sister to be called names, right?"

Ethan was puzzled for a moment but understood. "OK, I get it. You and Jack are very close friends."

"We are. But this ring really does have more meaning than just that." She gave A.C. Currant a look and then focused on her brother. "I don't know if this is the time or place to talk about my relationship with Jack." She glanced away, her eyes drifting to the winter darkness outside the window, looked back, straightened her shoulders, and calmly said, "I was dying. T.B. is nothing to mess with. Jack saved my life. And he cared for me. He found this apartment, and he got me a job with Mrs. Roosevelt. And...I am...I am very fond of him."

Ethan could sense the depth of his sister's feelings for Jack Travers. "I get it. Hey, we might have been able to return earlier, but Zak and I kind of screwed up with the *TimeTravelle.* That's one reason Dr. Currant is with us now. But there's another reason." Ethan sipped some brandy and then spoke slowly. "FDR is dead."

Emma made a face. "He is not. He won the election with the biggest turnout in history. I believe he's in the Bahamas right now on a fishing trip."

"You're right," said Currant. "He's still living at this moment. He's off with his Brahmin buddies living large. But he doesn't make it to the inauguration. He will be assassinated on February 15th. This is his future."

Emma's face registered the impact of the words. "No. It can't be. Everything's gone so well. Mrs. Roosevelt..." she dropped her head. "It's not fair," she mumbled. "It's not fair."

"Emma, I should tell you something. Dad is incredibly worried about you. We put him through the wringer with our rogue time-traveling. He told us to go back. To get you. And to return. He doesn't care about Roosevelt. He only cares about you."

"I care about Dad. But I also care about Mr. Roosevelt," she said quietly. "Millions of people in America care about him. He is the hope for the future."

Ethan inhaled deeply through his nose before speaking. "Zak and I found out some things going back to the future. Things you must know. The future sucks even worse than we knew, Emma."

Ethan then related their newfound knowledge about the deceptive reality they were living within in 2033. He told her about the underground cities and the massive elimination of citizens and explained that Mystic Heights was an isolated breeder town for midlevel worker bees.

"It's much worse than we thought. The world we thought we knew is dying, and there is no going back. There is no future."

"That's why we have to save him," she said. "He'll make the future better."

Currant took a sip of brandy and set down his glass. "Not half-bad, Emma. For Prohibition."

"Is that all you can say?"

"No. I have some ideas. You know, I have to agree with you on this one. I thought I could see my way to the end. Kind of close the door...or the casket lid, if you will...on my life and nostalgic memories of better times. But that's not right. Life...real human life...should go on. It will not unless we do something bold. And maybe the way to that end is to breathe some life into FDR's future. You three did it once; maybe we can all do it again."

Emma smiled. "I'm pleasantly surprised; I had given up on you. But I'm glad you're in the fight." She looked at Ethan. "I know Dad wants me home. He still thinks I'm his little girl. He's always been very protective. Especially after Mother died. But we have to do something. I'm not going anywhere until we figure this out."

"Well, then, let's see where we stand and what we can do," said Ethan. He turned to face Currant. "A.C., explain what's coming. Emma needs to know."

Currant looked pleased to have the floor. "So, as you said, Emma, FDR is alive and well at this moment. He's on Vincent Astor's yacht, probably having a grand time. Drinking, telling stories, and wrestling with the fish. And his inauguration is set for March 4th. But he'll only make it to the festivities if we clear the way for him. *The History* has him exiting the stage right in Miami just a few days from now. On the night of the 15th, he'll make a little speech in Bayfront Park, and thousands of people will come to see the President-elect that night. Then he'll be shot by an unemployed, crazy Italian immigrant named Zangara. We call him 'Mr. Z'. Sadly, FDR will die, and so will the Mayor of Chicago."

As Currant spoke, Ethan looked at his sister. This was becoming real for her now. Her face registered the immensity of the coming events. "We've got to tell Jack! We have to stop this from happening."

"Emma, listen to yourself," said A.C. His voice was calm, and his tone almost matter-of-fact. "Remember who we are," he continued. "You can't tell Jack anything. All of our lives depend on it."

"But..." she mumbled.

Currant's eyes narrowed. "He doesn't suspect. Does he?"

She shook her head. "Of course not. Do you think I've lost my mind?"

"What do I know? Sometimes people in a romantic situation give away their innermost secrets."

"That didn't happen. OK? Jack is a busy man. He really hasn't pried into my past. I've purposely let him glance at those monthly letters Ethan arranged to be sent to me at General Delivery. When he does meet you, he may ask what the heck took you so long to check in on your only sister. But that's it." She looked at A.C. "How do we explain you? Who are you supposed to be?"

Currant laughed lightly. "I will be your Uncle Arthur."

"Great," said Emma. "But I don't see the resemblance."

"By marriage, Emma. I am your father's late sister's husband."

"But he doesn't have a sister."

"He does now," said Currant, "his sister Ruth. Let's hope Jack Travers doesn't take the time to do some serious checking on us. We have enough *materia veritas* with us to display an appropriate background of our family. Just to make it believable."

They discussed their plans for another half-hour. Emma explained that her job with Mrs. Roosevelt involved interviewing ordinary people around the town. The President-elect's wife wanted to know how the real people handled the Depression. She and her husband were elitists and hopelessly removed from the reality of the nation's ordinary people. Emma met with people and wrote stories of their lives at the pace of about two or three a week. Then she submitted them to Mrs. Roosevelt via Jack Travers.

She told them that Jack had left his car in her care, that she now knows how to drive, and that she has a driver's license. Jack was out of town on business. She said he should be calling in tomorrow. After she checked in with Mrs. Roosevelt's aide and secured her approval, she agreed that she would tell Jack about her new plan. Her family and friends had arrived, and everyone would make a trip to Miami. It would be a vacation and an opportunity to interview some Southerners to give Mrs. Roosevelt additional insight. This would put them in Miami at the right moment for action, and Travers would remain in Washington. As Currant said: "It was a plan." Ethan and Zak thought it was a good plan. They believed they could stop the five-foot-tall, crazed Italian lone-assassin before he struck.

"How hard can it be?" signed Zak. "We know the day. We know the place and time. And we know the shooter. If a six-foot-five healthy American male and his super-strong good-looking friend can't stop some midget assassin, who can?"

"Don't forget Dallas. It may not be that simple," said Currant.

The time travelers nodded as they reflected on their unsuccessful 1963 mission.

Ethan wanted to speak to his sister in private. Since Ethan knew the 1930s and Washington, D.C., in detail,

Currant had no objection. He suggested Ethan return to the Mayflower no later than 10 o'clock as everyone needed to be fresh in the morning. Zak and Currant departed for the hotel.

Emma's apartment was quiet now, save for the crackling fire and pigeons cooing outside the window. Ethan and Emma sat side by side on the sofa. For a few minutes, they said nothing as they both stared into the dancing flames of the fireplace. He was glad to have a private discussion with his twin sister. Without showing it, he was shaken by the revelation of her engagement to Jack Travers, a man she had met only a few months earlier. The whole thing made little sense to him.

He spoke first. "You know, you're not very patient, Emma. We came back as soon as we could. Did you have to get engaged? You know this is an impossible situation. What were you thinking? That love would solve everything?"

She swiveled around and looked at him directly. "Oh, really? So you're an expert on love now? What the heck do you know about relationships between men and women? Have you ever even kissed a girl?"

"Of course," he said. "That's not the point."

"Right, you and your buddies pop off to some bar with some of the girls from school, and what? You end up with one for the night. Is that your idea of a loving relationship?"

Ethan got up and paced the floor. "OK. I admit I'm a little behind in that arena. But until our trip last year, I don't remember you ever getting serious with any guy. Anyway, that's your thing. I'm not talking about that. I'm thinking about what you've gotten yourself into. You're alive. We were all worried about you."

"Well, that's something. You just don't like my choice in men."

"What choice?" He looked down at her and shook his head gently. "You've hooked up with a man from the past. A man who doesn't exist in our world. You've created a relationship that can only lead nowhere. I mean, this whole thing is ridiculous. Do you love him?"

"There you go again. Flailing about." She gave him a determined look. He knew that look. She was digging in her heels. "What's it like to climb Mount Everest?"

"What? Have you had too much of that brandy? What are you talking about?"

"Exactly," she said. "You don't have a clue about love either, brother. Not one. Jack saved my life. I was dying of T.B. You know that."

"So you love him because he took care of you?"

"No, I just love him. Period. Maybe it will happen to you sometime. But I doubt it. Who would take you on?"

He remained silent.

A burning log crackled and popped a spark into the wire fireplace screen. Her face softened. "I'm sorry, Ethan. I didn't mean that. But if you think you're frustrated with this situation, think about me. I'm in love with a man more than a hundred years older than me. The only way I can be with him is to forgo my other life, my father, and you. It's impossible. But I'll tell you one thing. These last six months have been the best six months of my life. I've been with Jack. He's wonderful. I am playing an important role in shaping the history of America. I am alive. 1933 is alive. Truthfully, I almost feel like I could stay."

He sat down again on the sofa. This was not what he wanted to hear. "Come on, Sis. What about Dad? You would break his heart."

She looked into the flames again and waited several seconds before speaking. Her voice was weak. "I know. I know. Come here, you big idiot, and give me a hug. I'll need your help to get through this. And don't call me Sis."

He reached out and grabbed her shoulders, and pulled her to him. They held the hug until she pushed him away.

"All right, Mr. Answerman. What are we going to do next?"

Ethan thought before answering. "You'll have to work

things out with Jack. Is that possible?"

"Really, I have no idea. I don't want to go, but I can't stay. And I can't just get up and leave Jack. But we've got some time. A.C.'s machine is still on its twenty-eight-day cycle. Right?"

"So he says. Although he's not letting Zak or me know anything about the machine's workings. He was totally fried by our little excursion. That thing's his baby."

"For sure. But he's different now. More concerned and serious. If that's possible. What do you think?"

"I think he finally realizes he's getting old. His brother died...."

"What?"

"Yeah. I forgot you didn't know. He's gone. Died while we were away. It hit A.C. pretty hard."

"I'm sorry to hear that. But A.C. did give him a new life. Patrick would just be another sorry statistic in a police file without him. Anyway, I'm happy he's changed his opinion on remaking history for the better. Somehow I believe we already did it. Mr. Roosevelt will be a great leader, Ethan. If we can keep him alive."

"So Jack has gone to New York?"

"He's meeting with Mrs. Roosevelt. He won't tell me what it's all about, but I get the idea that it's serious stuff."

Ethan smiled. "Hey, we're right in the middle of things. Zak is full of piss and vinegar. A.C. Currant is on a mission. You're 100 percent healthy and facing the biggest challenge of your life. And I am ready to fix history. Let's face it. Our world of 2033 is in way worse condition than we ever suspected. As far as I know, we're the only people doing anything to make things better. Damn, it's exciting."

"I'll grant you that, brother. We're heading for Miami. Plenty of blue skies, bright sun, and palm trees."

"Right. And mobsters, assassins, and danger."

"Yeah," she said, "I hope we're ready for this."

Chapter IX-

The Assignment

The first month of 1933 was officially in the history books. Soon the people would have a new president; they would go back to guzzling alcohol, and life in the Great Depression might take a turn for the better. A few days ago, new First Lady Eleanor Roosevelt had summoned Jack Travers. He hadn't seen her face to face in over two months. On the afternoon of February 3, 1933, Jack took the train from Washington, D.C., to New York City. He spent the night in a hotel near the train station and departed for the run-up to Poughkeepsie the following day. His arrival just after noon was anticipated.

The driver took Travers' small suitcase and placed it in the backseat of the black Ford. Travers sat in the front passenger seat. Other than checking Jack's I.D., the driver maintained a low profile. He might have been a Secret Service agent, but Jack didn't inquire. Travers knew it was not productive to ask unnecessary questions about the people surrounding the Roosevelt family. The famous couple led complicated lives; sometimes, innocent questions posed to their minions could create the appearance of prying or strain the delicate social fabric woven by FDR and his family. The Roosevelts were above it all, and one didn't question those who helped maintain the grand illusion. Everyone just did their job.

The driver, a slender, well-groomed man in his late thirties, did not suffer small talk. Travers attempted to toss off a bit of innocuous banter, but the man only grunted in response. So Travers used the short ride from the train station to the Hyde Park complex as an opportunity to speculate. Two days ago, he got a call from Mrs. Roosevelt's secretary, who arranged the meeting. Jack was accustomed to this as Mrs. Roosevelt used him as a scout, a spy, a pulse-taker, and often a facilitator. He was an unofficial jack-of-all-trades, and she could rely on him to faithfully represent her husband's interests, and he was always available. But no topic had been revealed.

After FDR was elected, she spoke to Jack about the future. She intended her own efforts to benefit the people. She planned to become a very active First Lady of the United States. She knew her husband would help all the people, rich and poor, if he understood their needs. She recognized his physical handicap would limit his ability to personally experience their situations; therefore, she would become his eyes and ears.

In her mind, there was an unending supply of lobbyists representing the "special" interests of "special" people. She wanted to become a lobbyist for the average citizen. She envisioned a select group of people to act as extensions of her to do this. They would travel the country interviewing, writing about, and photographing Americans and everything they experienced.

In addition, she would actively establish a personal connection with the public. She wanted the best intelligence available. If she was to succeed as an active and influential First Lady, publically expressed opinions and actions would have to seamlessly integrate with her husband's. Good intelligence would provide a more precise focus, enhance FDR's image and, in general, allow both Roosevelts to make better decisions.

While Jack continued his intelligence gathering, his job became more important. Now, Mrs. Roosevelt relied on him to confidentially represent her in situations that would not permit her personal involvement. Jack Travers was, in some sense, an invisible "minister without portfolio." He held no title. He didn't work for any government agency. But now, he was a trusted member of Mrs. Roosevelt's inner circle. He worked directly for her. He was given specific authority to execute her intentions on a case-by-case basis. He was her facilitator, and he was becoming her friend. Given the urgency of her most recent request to meet with him in private, he was confident that he was about to become involved in something special.

The driver carefully turned off the main highway and drove onto a narrow road flanked by trees, with open expanses of snow-covered meadows to either side. This was Val-Kill, Eleanor Roosevelt's very private personal residence and retreat. Meeting her here was a first for Travers. He was entering her exclusive realm. Coming out of a turn, they approached a guard station on the side of the road. A large man wearing a leather jacket stood in the middle of the road. He waved them down. Although he obviously recognized the car and its driver, he came up to the passenger side window and studied Jack. He had a clipboard that held typewritten text and a photo. He glanced at the text and image.

"May I see your I.D., Mr. Travers?" Jack pulled out his wallet from his upper coat pocket, removed his driver's license, and handed it to the guard. The guard checked it against his information and then returned the card. "Fine, Mr. Travers. I'll ring the house and tell them you have arrived."

They drove on. The road twisted to the right. A frozen pond on the left fronted the modest one-story stone home. While the house had none of the comforts of the Roosevelts' townhouse in New York City or their nearby mansion on the Hudson River, it offered something more important to Mrs. Roosevelt—privacy and seclusion— two attributes that she cherished. The car circled around and stopped at the front entrance. Travers exited and stretched, releasing the tension in his body and mind. He took a deep breath. The air was fresh and cold. Except for a few birds chirping, there was a quiet emptiness. Jack looked beyond the vacant gardens and across the pond and icy fields. Blackbirds drifted up from the ground and flew across the sun. It was idyllic.

"Jack. There you are." Eleanor Roosevelt had a

peculiar, easily recognizable, high-toned schoolmarm voice, which didn't fit her personality. He turned, and she was in front of him. Her presence never ceased to impress him. At five-foot-eleven, she was one of the few women tall enough to almost look directly into his eyes. She was not a vision of beauty but had large, wide-set, welcoming blue eyes and a wonderful soul. In some son-to-mother way, he knew that he loved her. "You look wonderful," she said. Her broad smile welcomed him. "Did you have a good trip?" They shook hands.

"I did, Mrs. Roosevelt. Thank you."

She glanced over to the driver, smiled gently, and nodded. The man got back into the car. She and Jack strolled to the house. She held his arm and led him across the stone path to the cottage entrance. Inside, Jack was impressed by the simplicity of the space. Entering it was like being dropped into a brocaded handbag. It was warm, soft, and comfortable, decorated with vintage furniture and various personal artifacts; it was all woods and weaves, books, and bric-a-brac. They faced each other, sitting in wing chairs at the corner window near the fireplace. New logs flamed atop a layer of old burning coals. Bright winter sun coursed through the window glass and filtered through the sheer white curtains. Jack could feel the warmth of the sun's rays and enjoyed its calming presence.

"Some tea?" she asked as she waved her hand toward a side table on which a tea service had been placed.

"Yes. That would be nice. Long trip. But I'm glad to be here."

"Milk?"

He nodded. "A little."

She poured milk into both cups and filled them with hot tea. They sipped their tea for many minutes as they talked about Val-Kill. She touched on stories about the home and its importance to her. She enjoyed it. He had heard that her mother-in-law dominated her other homes, leaving her no room for self-expression or personalization. She said Franklin was traveling. He was in Warm Springs, Georgia, today, and tomorrow he would take the train to Florida for a fishing vacation. She was pleased her husband could have a respite before the inauguration as the campaign had been a grueling but rewarding experience. He deserved some time to play. She also mentioned that the two women who lived in the cottage were away for the afternoon. It appeared to Travers that she made a point to let him know they were alone in the house. In time, the conversation became more purposeful.

"Sorry to drag you up here from Washington, but unfortunately, Jack, I had no choice. We are about to confront a matter of grave importance."

"I'm honored to be here," he responded.

"And I am very pleased to hear that," she said, smiling.

Then she shifted in her chair, quiet momentarily, gathering her thoughts. Jack could sense that this was a complicated matter for her.

"I need not remind you that you must not discuss our conversation with anyone. What I tell you today is confidential."

Jack nodded. She had made this kind of introduction before. He no longer protested at her suggestion of the possibility that he would repeat any conversation between them. He simply sat, nodded, and listened.

"This is such an...unusual topic. One that is new to me. But we are talking about the worst type of people." She made a face. "I'm sorry. Let me begin at the beginning. As you may know, our son Jimmy..." she leaned her head back and then brought it down. Her eyes held a downward glance for a moment. "How shall I say it? He has a different outlook on life than his father and me. He hasn't found his grounding. Do you know what I mean?"

Jack nodded.

"He has become very close to Joe Kennedy. Kennedy is a man of money. He has been a generous supporter. For that, we are grateful. However, neither my husband nor I believe he is a proper role model for a young man. But Jimmy idolizes him. From his viewpoint, Kennedy is the epitome of a self-made man. He cavorts with Hollywood starlets and makes millions of dollars in the markets, and he lives on the edge of the underworld. All of this is very attractive to Jimmy. I guess that is natural. How does a boy make his mark in the world when his father is about to be the President of the United States? I understand that."

"Living in a shadow as large as that cast by Mr. Roosevelt could be difficult," said Jack.

"Yes. Maybe it is. But we all live in his shadow and in his radiance. As I said...I understand. A few days ago, Jimmy came to me with a story that is so very disturbing. He told me that Mr. Kennedy had revealed something as a personal favor to Jimmy and the entire family. You are probably aware that Kennedy has been trying to impress my husband for years. He would love to get a cabinet appointment. So we must keep this in mind when we evaluate his words. Jimmy said Joe Kennedy had been told by one of his friends in the liquor business that there would be trouble in Miami when Franklin returns from his fishing trip. Franklin is scheduled to give a short speech at an in-town public gathering on the evening of the 15th."

"What sort of trouble?"

"A shooting." She stopped herself at this point. Jack could tell she was moving into uncharted waters. She sipped her tea and took a moment to compose herself. "This 'friend' of Mr. Kennedy's is probably a mobster. But I have no doubt that this information is valid. Joe Kennedy would not gamble on his family's future by offering a fabrication. Have you heard of Frank Nitti? Of course, you know of him. You were in Chicago only a month ago. But you never mentioned him."

"I did not. However, I did some investigation. There is plenty of organized crime in Chicago, but as I discussed in my report to you, the street war will be over by the time the World's Fair opens. The winner will be too busy making money from the fair to do anything but maintain order. And so far as Mr. Nitti is concerned, I believe he's on his way out. Mayor Cermak is cracking down on the mobsters. Or at least some of them. He wants to drive Nitti and his gang out of Chicago well before the fair opening. Nitti's organization is...or maybe was...powerful. But the mayor has the entire police force at his disposal, and it is my understanding that he is supporting rival mobsters to help him oust the old Capone gang."

"That all makes sense, Jack. Except for the fact that the information that Jimmy related to me indicates that Mayor Cermak will be assassinated in Miami. The mayor is scheduled to participate in the ceremonies. I have been told that Nitti's people intend to kill the mayor when he comes to Miami." She took a deep breath.

"If this is so, why don't you alert the Secret Service?"

"The Secret Service protects the president. They do not protect anyone else. They will always protect the president. But this is not a threat to the president or even to the president-elect. My understanding is that it is only a threat to the mayor."

"But still... Do we know where this attack will take place?"

"We do not. I've told you what I know. Those mobsters could attack at any time and in any place in Miami. I think Mayor Cermak intends to be there for several days."

"And the mayor is not aware of this?"

"I've been told he has taken to wearing a bulletproof vest." She paused and looked into Jack's eyes. "Yes, he is well aware that he is a marked man. Apparently, he had one of his policemen shoot Mr. Nitti...unprovoked."

"Yes, I believe that is the case. Somehow Nitti survived. They found another of the mayor's mob associates dead about three weeks ago. A man named Newberry. So Nitti is out for revenge. It makes sense that he would try to kill Cermak in Miami. The Chicago police won't be there to protect him. And Miami is not exactly a bastion of civility. Who knows the allegiances of the Miami police? Do you know why Cermak needs to be in Miami?"

"It's all politics," she said. "He's looking for added Washington funding. Now that Franklin will be President, everyone is approaching him. Everyone wants to be his friend. The mayor also wants Franklin to open the Chicago World's Fair. But I know that will never happen."

"So Cermak knows his life is in danger. But there is nothing he can do. He must continue to play the game and hope for the best."

She sighed. "I guess that is the sum and substance of it, Jack. I just don't want any harm to come to my husband. We can't protect everyone. If Mayor Cermak wants to see my husband in Miami, that is an expression of his politics. We can put everyone on high alert. But so far as I know, there is no threat to my husband. This is a specific threat directed only at Mr. Cermak."

Jack Travers leaned back into his chair. He pursed his lips and looked directly into her eyes. "So what is your direction to me? What do you want me to do?"

She looked away from his gaze and simply sat in her chair, not moving a muscle. He waited. Slowly, she leaned forward as if someone in the empty house might hear her words. "I want you to fix it, Jack. I want to resolve the matter with those men in Chicago. I want them to understand that they must not place Franklin in danger. They must be aware that the government will bring vengeance upon their world if anything happens."

"So, you want me to meet with the assassination planners?"

"Yes," she said quietly.

Travers wanted to be sure of his authority. "And you are not telling me to stop them from trying to kill Mayor Cermak?"

"I am not. That is not our business. We cannot control everything, Jack. Our concern is for Franklin. Is that clear? I want you to meet with these people. Enlighten them and secure a clear understanding such that you can assure me that nothing will happen to my husband. Can you do that, Jack?"

Travers swallowed hard. "I mean no disrespect. But are you absolutely certain about this?"

"I am." Her voice was resolute, but her eyes were troubled and glistened.

"All right. I can do it. If you or your son can arrange the meeting."

"I have already discussed that with Jimmy, and he has cleared it with Mr. Kennedy. You will be notified."

"So be it." Jack Travers stood. He shook her hand. She did not appear to be in the mood to move, so he just bade her goodbye.

"Goodbye." Her voice trembled as she stared out the window. He wondered if she was already regretting her decision.

As he contemplated this latest assignment, he gazed out the car window on the return drive to the train station—frozen fields, a gray sky, and a storm on the horizon. Mrs. Roosevelt had placed him in a tough spot. Keeping Franklin Roosevelt alive was essential to many people, but he doubted the Chicago Outfit cared if Roosevelt lived or died. And he thought that the rich and powerful might be pleased to be rid of FDR. Roosevelt represented a threat to them, their way of life, and the future. J.P. Morgan, the DuPonts, the railroad tycoons, and many other sons and daughters of the robber barons of the Nineteenth century were now an elite aristocracy intent upon ruling the country with a president who served their interests, not the interests of the people. He could appear to be a man of the people. FDR could be a powerful and well-liked man, but he had to be controllable and always promote corporate interests, just like Hitler and Mussolini.

In this matter, Jack Travers knew he must proceed with caution. He would have to protect Roosevelt in a manner that would not reveal his own motivation.

-Chapter X-

The Outfit

Travers rode the train from Poughkeepsie to New York City. It arrived too late to catch the 20th Century Limited westbound to Chicago. In New York City, he checked into the new Savoy-Plaza Hotel. It might be a few days before he was notified of the meeting time and location; he wanted to be comfortable. That night he called Emma. She was excited because her brother, Zak, and an uncle had come to visit her. Jack was surprised at this news, only because of its abruptness. No warning. No phone calls. Now they all just pop in.

Emma had never really wanted to talk about her family. It seemed like this topic made her uncomfortable, so he never pressed. Now she was surrounded by family, and even more surprising, she asked if she could borrow his car to take a two-week trip to Florida. She said it would be good for her Uncle Arthur's health to get some sun, and she would take her interviews and write for the First Lady on location. Travers knew nothing of this plan. But he knew that compartmentalization was a big part of Eleanor Roosevelt's life from his dealings with her. This was between Emma and Mrs. Roosevelt.

He told Emma to take the car and have fun. He suggested he would join her in Florida if that was possible and that maybe they could meet in Miami. But Emma seemed reserved. Possibly she was uncertain about how to introduce him to her uncle. He realized that even in these modern times of the Thirties, the extent of his relationship with Emma was quite clear, and possibly some could suggest it was in bad taste. Old Uncle Arthur might be a puritanical New Englander. She told him she didn't know if they would get as far south as Miami but maybe Jacksonville. It all depended on her work and her interviews. She wanted to understand the plight of the poor on this trip through the South. Everything was unplanned but for that goal. Their conversation had ended with them agreeing to use Mrs. Roosevelt's secretary to connect. After they gushed out expressions of love and said goodnight, he hung up the receiver and smiled. Just hearing her voice made his day.

Travers' assumption about some delay in the meeting arrangements with the mobsters was correct. He would have two days of rest and relaxation. Late Monday, Mrs. Roosevelt's secretary gave him the phone number of a man in Chicago. The next day he boarded the 20th Century Limited. Traveling overnight across the country in a private compartment, he turned off the lights, removed his shoes, and reclined in an easy chair facing the window. He filled his glass with scotch whisky from his personal flask, lit a cigarette, and gazed out. The distant lights of farmhouses punctuated the night. When the steam train powered through a station at seventy miles per hour, the scene changed quickly to one of intense light and sound and then suddenly flickered back to the blackness and quiet of the countryside.

Traver's thoughts jumped to the task ahead. His image of Frank Nitti was garnered from newspaper photos; the man appeared dapper and mustached, with slicked-down hair, and—unlike the usual Chicago goon—he looked intelligent. And so he was, thought Travers. Al Capone, if nothing else, could judge a man's character. Before he went to prison, he chose Nitti to command his corporation. Frank Nitti was a man who could keep track of numbers. Nitti also recognized that the Prohibition gravy days would soon be over, and it was time to branch out in different directions. Although he was called "The Enforcer," Travers understood that he was a practical man who preferred the hum of a well-oiled business machine to the clamor of a Thompson submachine gun. However, this matter of Mayor Cermak was a life-or-death struggle; Cermak had the power to destroy the Outfit. So long as he was alive, Nitti would do anything to win the war.

As Travers sipped his drink, the porter knocked, entered, and prepared the bed. Shortly after that, Travers climbed into the berth and was lulled to sleep by the sound of the night train as it rolled west toward Chicago.

The train pulled into the LaSalle Street station at 7:59 the following day, and a few minutes later, Jack Travers made his call from a phone booth in the waiting room. Nitti's attorney, de Stefano, was quick and to the point. Travers told him he would be staying at the Stevens. The attorney agreed to get back to him today. Early afternoon, while Travers was eating lunch in his room, he received a call asking him to wait out front on Michigan Boulevard. Someone would come by in fifteen minutes to drive him to the meeting.

As he stood at the curb, a new Cadillac pulled up. The well-dressed young man driving asked if he was Mr. Travers. "That's me," he said, getting in. There was another not-so-pretty man in the backseat. Travers didn't get a good look at him, but it was enough to tell him he was a goon. The driver turned right at the next street. Two blocks later, he pulled over and stopped the car. He reached into his coat pocket and pulled out a black blindfold. He handed it to Travers. "Sorry, but you have to wear this. Orders."

Travers was about to laugh, but he remembered the man sitting behind him. He slipped on the blindfold and sat quietly with his hands folded in his lap. He was used to flying blind. Mentally, he added this journey into the unknown to the dozens of others he had taken in his life. It's all part of the fun, he thought. Not more than twenty minutes later, the car stopped. Someone opened the door for him.

"We're here. Get out, and I'll walk you in," said the driver. The man guided him along a walk, down six steps, and then patted him down for weapons. He heard the sound of a key in a lock. The door opened, and he was guided in. "You can remove your blindfold now, Mr. Travers."

In the small, darkened, windowless room, Travers squinted. He assumed he was in the basement of a house.

"Have a seat," the driver said as he waited for him to sit on the old sofa. Travers watched him squeeze past the goon standing outside as the man exited. The door was locked. Travers smelled mold. He didn't like sitting on the sofa; something might seep into his suit. He stood and waited. Soon, another man entered the room from the other door. It wasn't Nitti. The man wore a black suit and tie and was of medium height, dark-haired, and young. Travers guessed he was in his early twenties. A cigarette dangled from his lips.

"Welcome to Chicago, Mr. Travers. My name is Saul Alinsky." His voice was resonant and smooth like honey-soaked smoke. His face, fleshy, olive-toned, smiled at Travers. They shook hands. "Smoke?" he asked.

"No, thanks. I'm perpetually quitting."

Alinsky smiled. "Vices are like undesirable friends. Sometimes appealing and maybe even addicting, but vices nevertheless."

Travers returned the smile, and the two men eyed each other without speaking. Alinsky looked like a college student or maybe a teacher. He was self-assured, young, and on the make, and he had a distinctive second-generation Ellis Island look. Both men were comfortable with the moment of silence. Alinsky broke the spell.

"I'm an acquaintance of Mr. Nitti. He has asked me to greet you." He took another drag from his cigarette, blew out the smoke, and snuffed out the cigarette in the metal-and-glass ashtray standing next to the sofa. "We'll meet with him shortly. You know he is recovering from several gunshot wounds?"

"Yes, I read about that."

"Actually, it's remarkable he survived. His will to live is extraordinary. But we do need to respect his time. Tell me, Mr. Travers, why are you here?"

Jack Travers wavered. "I would prefer to speak to Mr. Nitti regarding the reason for my visit."

Alinsky smiled, this time without exposing his teeth. "I'm sure you would. But you and I must have our discussion first. If you are unwilling to talk to me, I will have to ask the man outside to take you back to your hotel."

Travers decided not to press the matter. He was in the lion's den with a goon outside one door and the unknown behind the other. "I'm here to talk about Miami. This is where our interests cross."

"You mean the interests of Mr. Roosevelt and Mr. Nitti. Correct?"

"I'll be blunt. We have been told that an assassination has been planned. That Mayor Cermak is the target. And that this event will occur in Miami."

"You are aware that the men who shot Mr. Nitti were working for the mayor?" asked Alinsky.

"That was my assumption."

Alinsky circled the room, talking as he walked. "So we have a conflict here. You want to protect the next President of the United States; Mr. Nitti wants to stop a man who wants to kill him and destroy his organization." He stopped walking and looked directly at Travers. "Conflict is good, Mr. Travers. It quickly clarifies the situation. I take it you have the authority to speak for Mr. Roosevelt."

"Concerning this matter, and this matter alone, I do." Travers smiled. "The family sees this proposed action in Miami as a threat to them and their interests. They have sent me here to resolve this matter."

"I like a man who knows his limitations. And I say that with all due respect. Come with me."

Travers followed Alinsky through the door into a corridor leading to a massive hardwood stairway. Saul Alinsky made his way up the stairs, glancing back occasionally to check on his charge. They entered a rectangular hall at the top with paneled doors at each end and two sliding doors facing them in the middle. A skylight flooded the space with natural light. One step into the hall, Alinsky stopped, as did Travers. Then Alinsky did a strange thing. He pulled out his cigarette lighter and tapped the wood handrail behind him; he tapped loudly three times, waited, and tapped twice. The sliding doors parted. A heavy-set, dark-skinned man with a pock-marked face looked at Travers and Alinsky. He held a revolver and waved them ahead with his free hand.

The cavernous space might have been a dining room at one time. The walls were covered in dark wood paneling, and high windows hugged the ceiling. Frank Nitti, wearing a soft red silk robe over black silk pajamas, lay on a sofa at the end of the room. His lower half was covered with a blanket. Travers noticed he had shaved his mustache. The head of Chicago's Outfit looked very small and frail on the large sofa, his head and shoulders propped up by some decorative cushions.

He motioned to Travers to sit. Alinsky and Travers sat in two chairs facing Nitti. Behind them, the man with the gun closed the sliding doors and stood like a soldier watching Travers. His revolver had found a temporary home under his armpit in a holster.

"I'd stand up, Travers, but some lousy cops tried to kill me. I'm stuck on this sofa." He looked at Alinsky. "I see you've met the Professor." He waited for Travers to comment.

"I did. We had a nice conversation downstairs."

"Right. He's good with the gab. College boy. Studying us for his research paper. Like little rats in a cage. But I enjoy his company. He's a pleasant diversion from the typical jerks I deal with. We get along. I amuse him, and he amuses me. Ain't that right?"

"That is true, Mr. Nitti."

"OK. Now. Jack Travers. Let's talk." He lifted his upper body and slid higher on the sofa. He groaned audibly. "Jesus. Those bastards," he said under his breath, but loud enough for all to hear. "I understand some of our blabbermouth friends out East have been telling stories about our little world here in Chicago. OK. So you and your boss know what we're up to."

Travers fidgeted in his chair. "Mind if I smoke?"

Nitti laughed. "I don't give a shit what you do. But I wouldn't make any sudden moves, or my friend over there might get excited. "Saul, why don't you give Mr. Travers a cigarette and have one yourself. I'd have one with you, but my good doctor says it's bad for my health." He laughed and then coughed involuntarily. "That's a joke."

Travers smiled and nodded. He noted Nitti's look of pain during the short coughing fit.

"I suppose you figured out what's happening here? You get it. Right?"

"I see that very clearly. I can say there is no doubt out East that you have been wronged. But my people do not have opinions to express regarding your differences with the current local administration."

Nitti smiled. "You two should get together," he said, eyeing Travers and Alinsky. "Same charm school. You could give each other word massages. Go on. Your turn to talk." He adjusted his robe to close off the view of his damaged chest area.

"Well…"

Nitti cut him off. "Sorry, Travers. But get out whatever you have to say. I'm hurtin'. I can't sit around and B.S. forever."

Travers straightened up. "Right. I'll get to the point. Mr. Roosevelt is scheduled to visit Miami on the 15th. I understand Mr. Cermak will be in attendance."

"A happy coincidence," said Nitti with a smile.

"Yes. Our only goal is to have Mr. Roosevelt make his visit safely and leave. That is all. We are asking you to make sure that happens."

"Or what?" asked Nitti. His face reddened.

Saul Alinsky interrupted. "Mr. Travers. You are not

attempting to direct Mr. Nitti, are you?"

Travers looked at him and took his cue. He spoke to Nitti directly. "Of course not. Your business is your business. While we do not wish violence upon anyone, it's not an ideal world. You must protect your interests as we must protect ours. Mr. Roosevelt will soon become the most powerful man in the world. That said, every man is mortal. And every man must have friends. And men in power always have enemies. While I cannot promise Mr. Roosevelt's friendship, I can offer his tacit acknowledgment of those who make it possible for him to do his job. The coming years will be a challenge for him and for the country. We all have more problems than we can handle. But I can assure you that you are not one of his problems. You can help him by allowing him safe passage in Miami, and for that, you will have his respect." Travers knew he was stretching his authority, but he wanted to get a commitment.

Nitti was quiet for a moment. "So you're sayin' you don't have a dog in this fight? Is that right?"

"That's right."

"And our business in Miami won't be interfered with?"

"Correct."

Nitti smiled. "OK. I get it, Jack. I'm a businessman. Good business makes sense to me. Nobody who has half a brain really wants trouble. Any trouble. This is a growin' city, and ours is a growin' business. My business is here in Chicago. Some Washington guys have made trouble for us in the past. It would be nice to know that respect you talk about would cause some...what would you call them...courtesies to be extended to us."

Travers' eyes darted up and to the left, then back down to Nitti.

"That discussion, Mr. Nitti, is beyond me. But certain things are obvious. I think the goals of my principal and yours are not conflicting."

Nitti smiled. "More fancy talk. Just like you, Professor. I love it." He turned back to Travers. "Come here."

Jack Travers rose slowly and involuntarily looked over his shoulder at the guard at the door.

"Don't be so squeamish. I just want to shake on it."

Travers leaned into the injured mob boss.

Nitti started to speak but lost his voice temporarily. "Time to go, Travers," he whispered. "So your people won't get in our way in Miami?"

"Our people are there to protect Mr. Roosevelt. That is their charge."

"No interference?"

"Not from us, but I will say it seems everyone in the country knows of your intentions. I only speak for our people. For the record, I may find myself in Miami. Just to observe."

"It's a free country, but don't make waves. Except maybe when you go to the beach, eh?" He chuckled to himself and coughed.

"It's part of my job to be there."

"Well, I got a guy. Dave Yaras. He'll be keeping an eye on you. Miami is a dangerous place. He'll make sure you stay out of trouble."

"I'll remember that."

"Shake on it like we both mean it. Nothin' bad will happen to your boy from anything we do. And anything we do is our business. Right?"

"That's exactly correct, Mr. Nitti. Exactly."

"*Oro è che oro vale*," said Nitti with a wry smile. They shook hands, and he waved them off with a groan.

After returning to the basement room, Alinsky handed him the blindfold. "It's been my experience that all real progress is made in reaction to a threat, Mr. Travers. I think you have made some progress today."

"I hope so," said Travers.

"But the threats are real. Remember Teddy Newberry? Years ago, he worked for Bugs Moran. More recently, he became the mayor's bagman. I believe he ordered those cops to shoot Mr. Nitti. I think he thought he was powerful. Because he was at the right hand of Cermak. But he's dead now. In this town, swift justice is the order of the day."

Jack Travers realized this man, Saul Alinsky, was someone to remember—not a mobster, but still dangerous. He pursed his lips but offered no response.

"Very shortly, everything will be settled here. Mayor Cermak has made some bad decisions. He will have to face the consequences of those. Chicago will have a new mayor. I know who that will be. That man will be solidly behind your boss and have no issues with Mr. Nitti. As you said, this country has enough problems to fix without creating new problems. All people have issues, and everyone has problems to be managed. It's up to each of us to make decisions and move forward. This is just my opinion, but you can tell Mr. Roosevelt for me that everyone here in Chicago wishes him nothing but success. This country needs some fresh blood."

"That it does, Mr. Alinsky," said Jack Travers. Dirty business, he thought as he focused on the word 'blood,' knowing that Anton Cermak's blood was destined to stain the streets of Miami.

"Call me Saul." Alinsky smiled, exposing a mouth full of teeth like a mean chimpanzee.

"Goodbye, Saul." They shook hands. Travers put on his blinders and left.

-Chapter XI-

On the Road Again

"Just like our trip to 1963," said A.C. Currant. He sat in the passenger seat of Jack Travers' 1930 Buick roadster. The rain had stopped, and the convertible top was down. Zak and Ethan sat in the rumble seat. They drove along a two-lane concrete highway in southern Georgia, heading south to Florida, Emma at the wheel. She was the only one with a real driver's license, so it was decided to give her most of the driving duties. Currant was not taking chances on this trip. He did not want a run-in with the law and knew that contact between the average person and police was most likely to occur on the road. Emma didn't mind driving. She was an accomplished driver now and liked the freedom of cruising down the highway. Traffic was light. She thought about Jack, wondering what he was doing and if he was really coming to Florida. Her last conversation with Mrs. Roosevelt's secretary was yesterday, the third day of their road trip. Jack had left her a message. He would take the train down to Miami as soon as his business in Chicago had been completed. Of course, she looked forward to seeing him again, even though it posed problems that weighed heavily upon her.

Jack's attention would have to be diverted while Ethan and the others attempted to track down the assassin, Zangara. She remembered what Ethan had told her. According to *The History*, Giuseppe Zangara was thirty-two years old and an unemployed mason living in Miami. He had no connection to organized crime. He suffered from stomach pains and blamed his deplorable social and physical conditions on those in power. For Zangara, it made no difference who was in control; they were all blood-sucking leeches who cared nothing for the little man. Allegedly he shot and killed Franklin Roosevelt because FDR was a leader. Of course, at the moment, FDR was between jobs; he had no governmental power. He was awaiting his inauguration. Herbert Hoover was the current leader of the land. But, no matter, Zangara's tummy hurt so badly that he killed Roosevelt before he could prove himself to either little or big people. When she thought about it, the whole scenario seemed crazy. But then again, Zangara was supposed to be crazy, so somehow, the logic was foolproof.

"Emma, my dear. You are ignoring me," said Currant in a louder voice.

She heard him this time. "Sorry, I was just thinking about the road ahead."

"And I was saying that this trip reminds me of our trip to 1963. Driving around the South, spending time in New Orleans and Dallas. And just having fun."

"Oh. Right, A.C. That was fun watching JFK get his head blown off. And you shooting at airplanes."

She looked to her right. Currant was well-tanned and looking pretty good for an old man. He chuckled as his long gray-streaked hair flew about in the wind. "Come on. We had fun. You've got to admit it. You love going back, don't you?"

She nodded. "I do. Actually, I'm quite taken by the times. I understand why you built your machine now. It was for your benefit, wasn't it?"

"Who else? Who's more important than me?"

She shook her head. "You're impossible, 'Uncle Arthur.'"

"You remembered."

"I'm practicing. And you should, too. We'll soon be meeting Jack, and we have to sell the big lie."

"That should be easy, Emma. I've always been like an uncle to you. Sweet and caring. Attentive and loving...."

"Stop it. Remember your own first rule of selling. Don't oversell!"

"You have a point." He looked back to eyeball the two

in the rumble seat behind him. "OK, back there?

Ethan swatted his forehead. "Except for the bugs in my teeth, everything's fine." Zak just gave a thumbs-up to Currant and smiled.

Emma focused on the road, ignoring her passengers. Traveling to Florida in 1933 by car was a bit of a challenge. Some roads were new and in excellent condition. Still, others, particularly those they encountered on side trips to gather material for her stories of the Great Depression, were nothing more than rutty dirt trails into the wilderness. Emma discovered that workers on the tobacco plantations in North Carolina and in the cotton fields of South Carolina and Georgia were dying of starvation. They lived in subhuman conditions without toilet facilities, electricity, or running water. Migrant-worker parents would work the fields during the day, leaving young children to shelter themselves under cardboard, tin, and canvas constructs unsuitable for animals. She was amazed at the extent of poverty that beset these people of the rural South. They had little, to begin with, but now amid an economic depression and year after year of pounding hurricanes, falling prices, crop and animal disease, and disheartening and disruptive farm consolidation and mechanization, these "little people" had little to cheer about. Sharecroppers and migrant workers were invisible citizens without voices. She intended to make their voices heard through her written reports to Mrs. Roosevelt. The new president would make changes to help these poor souls, the Bonus Marchers, and everyone who was jobless, hungry, and helpless.

Her mind drifted back to last August and time spent with the Sweeny family in the most famous Hooverville, Camp Marks, on the banks of the Anacostia in Washington, D.C. She wondered what had happened to Mrs. Sweeny and her family. They had survived the attack by Hoover's army, but had they found a way to live after that horrible evening when the Bonus Marchers' camp went up in flames? After recovering from her illness, she tried to find them, but they were gone, like most of the Marchers. She hoped Mr. Roosevelt would help them, but now she knew many Americans were without. She interviewed some of these people and kept notes in a bound book of blank pages. Her recordings of their misery and deprivation would eventually be delivered in her reports to Mrs. Roosevelt. For the first time in her life, she was doing important work. This pleased her. She had a mission to listen to the faint heartbeat of a dying America.

Miles of dusty farms rolled by as the Buick traveled south at a steady forty miles per hour. They found a roadside café about fifteen miles from the Georgia-Florida border, and this gave them all time to decompress and rejuvenate. Simple platters of fried chicken, biscuits, and gravy were tasty, unlike any food served in 2033. Afterward, they rested on the front porch of the café. Two beat-up wooden chairs and a two-person wooden swing provided ringside seats for a still-life painting of 1933 rural America. Zak and Emma swung gently while Ethan and A.C. Currant leaned back in their chairs. Ethan drank from a bottle of cola, making happy noises after each gulp. Currant had purchased a corncob pipe and some tobacco. The aromatic smoke filled the hot, still, midday air and mixed with the pervasive smell of old wood, manure, and turned earth. Insects buzzed.

But for the occasional car that swished by on the highway, the scene was quiet. The sun beat down on the two old-fashioned glass-flask gas pumps that stood like silent sentinels between them and the road. The Buick, the top in place to keep the sun off its leather seats, was the only car in the lot. A mangy black dog wandered through the scene. With his tongue laid out like a floppy hat, he loped along, seemingly unaware of the presence of Northerners. Zak broke the silence when he slapped his hands together on a bug. Ethan took a final swig of his soda and set the bottle on the floor next to his chair.

"Hey Emma," he asked. "Are we done with our social studies work?"

"Don't mock me. What I'm doing is important. The more information Mr. Roosevelt has, the more problems will be solved after he takes office. Our old buddy Herbert Hoover hasn't done a thing. You can see that."

"Your supposition might be correct, but only if FDR remains alive. We have important work in Miami," said Ethan.

"I'll still be taking the pulse of the people there. I need to get the city perspective," she said.

Currant sucked on his pipe, straightened up in his chair, and snorted out a lungful of smoke as if he had awakened from a dream. "Got to get going, gang. We're running out of time. We only have a week to get to Miami, find the crazed killer, and stop him from doing his deed. You well remember the last time we attempted this. We failed." He cocked his head. "Think we'll get any help from Jack?"

Emma frowned. "I don't know. He might know something about the security arrangements, but we'll have to be circumspect in our questioning."

"Can he get us close to the action?" asked Ethan.

She thought. "Jack works for Mrs. Roosevelt. I don't know. We might have to focus on keeping him out of our way. He has no idea that FDR is under threat."

"Think we better pick up this conversation in the car, guys." Zak pointed to the open windows of the café. *"Let's get into our breezer and move on."*

"A.C., we have to switch now. My legs are really getting cramped. That rumble seat is not designed for me. You and Zak are a better fit," said Ethan.

"Two midgets might work," signed Zak. *"It's not really built for adults."*

"After we cross the border," said Currant, "I'll drive, and Emma, you spend some time with Zak. OK?"

"I'm good with that. I'm getting tired of driving. I'd like to nap on Zak's shoulder," said Emma.

Zak smiled.

Seating arrangements in place, they headed back to the car, piled in, and took off for Florida.

A half-hour later, Emma slowed the car as they pulled up to a line of vehicles.

"This is the state line," said Currant. "Must be a roadblock."

"Do you think they're looking for us?" asked Ethan.

"What are you talking about?" said Emma.

Ethan shrugged. "I don't know. I'm just getting gun-shy. Zak was right—too much loose talk back at the café. We have to remember that we are foreigners...from the North. We sound and look weird to these people. And even before we meet them, they don't trust us."

"You're right about that," said A.C. Currant. "We're outsiders, and outsiders are suspicious by definition. At least we're not crossing into Mississippi. They might string us up for sport. Those guys really don't like Northerners. Remember, the Civil War ended just sixty-five years ago. That's a New York minute to the Confederates."

"Spoken like a true Yankee, Uncle Arthur," said Emma.

The line moved slowly. A car at the front turned around and drove back past them. Emma checked the radiator temperature. "Next time we stop for gas, remind me to get water," she said quietly. It was a roadblock. Concrete barriers lined the side of the road, and a sign on a sawhorse read: *Be Prepared To Prove You Live Here.* A black-and-white police car sat on the road's shoulder. Behind the car, a large beach umbrella planted in the ground offered the cop refuge from the sun. The young uniformed man looked hot, red-faced, and sweaty. As Emma slowly pulled up, he blocked the road with his person and came around to her side.

"Afternoon, miss." He looked at the other occupants in the car. "Gentlemen..."

"Good afternoon, officer," said Currant.

He put one foot on the running board. "Driver's license."

She dug the cardboard evidence out of her purse and handed it to him.

He looked at it carefully. "Washington, D.C. Just visiting the Sunshine State, or are ya'll looking for work?"

She smiled at him. His face was close now, and he was taking in the view. She did her best Bette Davis imitation, wiggling her body slightly and watching his eyes. "We're traveling to Miami to get a break from the Northern weather. Just looking for some fun and sun. Thankfully, we don't need a job. That we have. Is that all right, officer?"

He smiled and paused to admire her. "That's just fine. We do like tourists, Miss. Just don't have any extra jobs available. That's how it is. Go on. Ya'll drive ahead and have a good time in Miami." He returned her license, which she handed to Ethan. The cop backed off the running board and stood tall, admiring the view. She swung her head back and smiled at the cop. "Thank you, officer. Have a wonderful day," she said sweetly.

He grabbed the bill of his cap, smiled, and then moved to the car behind them.

As they motored ahead, the wind cleared the gathered heat, and they leaned back in their seats and sighed. "Not much of a welcoming committee for anyone looking for a job," said Ethan.

"That's the point. There are no jobs," said Currant.

That night they stayed in a tourist camp outside Stuart, Florida. They had hoped to make it to Miami, but that was three hours away. They paid for two cabins and spent the night. After filling the radiator and gassing up the following day, they continued. Mid-day, they rolled into Miami. Approaching downtown, they drove along the vast expanse of Biscayne Boulevard. Soon Bayfront Park filled the view to their left, and the prestigious waterfront hotels lined the boulevard to their right. They arrived at the McAllister Hotel.

After they parked, Ethan looked toward Bayfront

Park. "Isn't that where Roosevelt is scheduled to die?"

"We have to work on that little problem, don't we?" said Currant.

"Remember, the guy is only five feet tall!" Zak signed.

LOG of Zak Newman
February 8, 1933 (local time): 23:37 (Day 7 of time travel)

We finally arrived in Miami, and I'm happy to be here. The weather's great—about 78 degrees and sunny. A.C. Currant and I share a room six floors up, overlooking the ocean. At this moment, a warm, salty breeze is wafting through the window next to my writing desk. Sure beats the frozen mess we left in Mystic Heights. This town is like a boxer who was knocked down and took a nine-count. The Great Depression started early for Miami. The real estate boom crashed in the mid-'20s, and in late 1928 a hurricane blew through Florida, killing about 10,000 people. Then a freeze hit, destroying crops; insects took over, knocking out the citrus crops. By the time the stock market crashed in 1929, Miami was already on the canvas. But now the town is beautiful— all-white buildings and green tropical plantings. It appears to have recovered. The racetracks, both horses and dogs, are operating. The hotels are full of tourists.

Of course, crime is still big business. From what I understand, this is an "open city," which means no specific group of mobsters controls the gambling industry. Apparently, gambling is illegal, but only on a technical basis. Punch cards, bingo, slot machines, card games, and dice games were just a few of the possibilities suggested by our bellboy on his way out the door. Who knows? Maybe we will place a few bets on a dog. That would be fun. Currant says he will need to refill the coffers soon. So maybe a trip to the track will be in order.

Tomorrow we have our reunion with Jack Travers. Our backstories are ready. Hopefully, our phony history will ring true. I'm not real thrilled about Jack's relationship with Emma. Neither is Ethan. But he was there for her when she needed help, and he watched over her while we were gone. Ethan assures me that she'll return back home with us. And we're all on the same page when it comes to saving Mr. Roosevelt. The tricky part will be saving him while Jack Travers is watching. Maybe Emma can keep him occupied while Ethan, Currant, and I stop the assassination.

Where do we start? We know the killer's name, and we know the place and time: Zangara, Bayfront Park, 9:35 p.m. on Wednesday, February 15, 1933. The park is right across the street from our hotel. So everything is very convenient for our little group of dragon slayers. All we have to do is find the crazy little dragon and put out his fire. I guess the other feature of this venture is that we will have to remain anonymous heroes. We must somehow stop the little man without drawing attention to ourselves. Our backstories and phony identification would never withstand public exposure as national heroes. Maybe we can make Jack Travers the hero. Or maybe there won't even be a hero. Suppose we can just interrupt the flow of events sufficiently to permit FDR to make his speech and get out of town. In that case, the crime will never be committed, FDR will be inaugurated, and the future of America may be forever changed for the better.

We can hope. We have one week to do our magic—in Magic City.

End 02-08-33

-Chapter XII-

Meet the Family

"Nice to meet you, Uncle Arthur. If I may call you that," said Jack Travers.

A.C. Currant shook hands with him. "I prefer A.C., Jack. You can call me A.C. In fact, everyone, including Emma, calls me A.C."

"OK, A.C., it is." Jack smiled. "Well, we're all back together, and Emma's hitting on all sixes now. Completely healed. And of course, you know, Emma and I are engaged."

Ethan nodded. "That was surprising news. You're a fast worker, Jack Travers."

Zak's hands itched to talk; Emma saw the look in his eyes. She hoped he would keep his comments to himself. Only he had remained stubbornly inelastic about her relationship with Jack. She grabbed Jack's arm and drew him closer. "Jack has been my guiding light and chief nurse for the past six months. I don't know what I would have done without him." She smiled lovingly at Travers. I've got myself a handsome man, she thought to herself. Ethan and Zak will just have to learn to live with it. If nothing else, A.C. Currant seemed to be unconcerned about her relationship. Her opinion of him moved up a notch or two. Ethan told her he had changed. So it seemed.

"Well, should we grab lunch?" asked Currant.

Zak signed quickly. *"Now you're talking, A.C. I'm starving."*

"You and me both, amigo," said Ethan. "As they say in Japan, *tabe masho.*"

They ate their lunch at the hotel restaurant, outside facing the bay. The time-travelers were careful not to discuss current events or their lives at home. Currant focused the conversation on Jack and Emma's work, letting them do most of the talking. Every so often, he would bring up a topic related to the world of physics in 1933, but Jack only seemed mildly interested, which was OK with Emma.

"So, Jack, are you excited about the upcoming inauguration?" asked Currant. "I heard on the radio that they have finalized the electoral vote. It's official now. Surprise...FDR is the winner," he laughed. "Will you attend?"

"I'm afraid not, A.C. I'm strictly a behind-the-scenes kind of guy."

"Too bad," said Currant. "I would really like to meet Franklin Roosevelt."

"I would too," said Jack. He looked thoughtful for a moment. "That would be the highlight of my career."

"But you have met Mrs. Roosevelt?"

"Of course, she's a lovely lady."

"Emma, you met the boss last year," said Ethan. "You must have made quite an impression. She hired you."

Emma blushed. "I doubt that. I think I owe my good fortune to Jack. But I'm hoping to see her again the next time she's in Washington." She looked at Travers again. "Jack. After lunch, can we go for a walk by the water?"

"That would be wonderful, dear," he said.

Emma noticed that Zak winced when he heard the word "dear."

Later, Currant and Jack argued politely about who would pay the bill, but Currant insisted that he pick up the tab. He did, and they split up. The boys and Currant went for a walk downtown, and Emma and Jack headed for Bayfront Park. Crossing to the center of Biscayne Boulevard, they looked down the colonnade of palm trees. Rows of lush tropical flowers filled the lawns with color.

"This is truly a beautiful place. It's just like a movie," Emma said.

"Even better. It's in color," Jack quipped. "I'm so glad you could come down to visit. I'll be here at least for a week. How about you?"

"Yes, we will too."

"And you are doing interviews?"

"Right," she smiled, "and just fooling around."

He leaned over and kissed her lightly. "Fooling around?"

"Jack, now be a good boy. Someone could be watching."

"I hope they get an eyeful. I'm not ashamed of my feelings for you, dear."

She laughed, and they walked on. Strolling along the water's edge, the bright Miami sun comforted them. They purchased a couple of Italian ices from a cart vendor and slowly drifted along the walk, watching the boats dart about in the bay. They came to the band shell and seating area at the end of the path. The open stage was covered by a round roof attached to a boxy building capped with two onion domes.

"It's almost certain Mr. Roosevelt will be speaking here."

"Oh, really," Emma said. "I hadn't heard that. Maybe we will see him then."

"Yes," said Travers." His eyes drifted from the expansive semi-circular seating area to the stage. He paused. "I'm sure we will."

She gazed at him as the sun bounced off his bronzed face and clean-cut mustache. His aviator sunglasses reflected the multicolored scene but hid his eyes. "At least a penny for your thoughts."

He returned from his mind-drifting. "Sorry...I've got an idea. Let's sit in the rock garden, and we can talk. If the frogs aren't too loud. All right?"

She nodded and squeezed his hand playfully.

They retraced their steps and entered the distinct realm of the rock garden. The play of dark green and light green foliage above filtered sunlight onto the path, animating their walk as the sounds of birds hidden in the trees filled the air. A quiet reflecting pond beckoned, a light wind rippled the green water, and lily pads floated and danced on the surface. They settled onto a shaded bench facing the pond. Side by side, this time, they kissed for real. Emma felt the passion in her rise. She caught her breath before speaking. "This reminds me of the first time we kissed at the Lincoln Memorial. Remember?"

He laughed. "You think I'd forget the day I fell in love?"

"No," she mumbled as she dropped her head. She remained silent.

"What's up?"

She looked at him and then carefully removed his sunglasses, folding and placing them in the front pocket of his jacket. "I have to go back, Jack."

He nodded. "I figured as much. How long?"

"I don't know. My father is not feeling well," she lied. "I'm not sure. But I'll come back as soon as I can. Will you wait for me?"

"Come on, Em. It's not forever."

She kissed him on the cheek. "You're right. I'm being silly," she said as she drifted back into silence.

"What's bothering you?"

"I was thinking about us. I have a question."

"About what?"

"About my stay in the hospital. It's been on my brain for months. When I found out I had TB, I was really in a bad way. I had the feeling that I wouldn't make it. I was weak, but I still remember the nurses' faces when I asked them about my chances. They were always upbeat, but their faces couldn't lie. But you came every day. And every day, you gave me a pill, and I recovered fairly quickly. I know the doctors were amazed at my recovery. But I wasn't. I knew I would live. Because I trusted you."

"It was a miracle, Emma," Jack said. "I was there for you then, and I'm here now."

Emma pulled away gently and looked into his eyes. "It really wasn't a miracle, was it, Jack? I never told them about your pills, but I'm certain you were the one who cured me. Not the doctors and not a miracle. So that's my question, Jack. What was in those pills, and where did you get them?"

Jack looked out onto the water for a long time. Finally, he spoke. "Emma, you have to promise me you will tell no one. Not even your brother."

"Some things are just for us, Jack. I know that."

"You know I am a bit of an insider. I have friends in high places."

"Sure."

"Well, I was desperate when you became ill. It looked as if you were going to be gone forever. You're right. The doctors were not encouraging at all. They told me to prepare for the worst." He shook his head. "I wasn't ready for that. I went to Mrs. Roosevelt. I told her about you. Even then, she was quite taken with you. I pleaded with her for help. Anything. She understood completely. When her husband was stricken with the polio disease, she tried every avenue, every doctor and clinic. She became an expert on the subject of poliomyelitis. But becoming an expert did not make a difference. In time, her husband did stabilize. But there was no hope for a remission of his disease. However, I knew she had extensive contacts in the world of medicine. It was through those contacts that I received that medicine. I have no idea what it was. Maybe I'll never know, but it did work. You are the living proof."

"So why not everyone? Why me?"

Jack raised his shoulders. "First, it was an experimental drug. Second, it only existed because it came from a world in which you and I do not live. A world of money and power. I have no idea where it actually came from. It was delivered to me by a special messenger. Mrs. Roosevelt, while pleased with your recovery, never mentioned her role, if any, or my receipt of the pills. No one has ever asked me about their effectiveness. So you see, Emma, it was a miracle in a very real way." He smiled. "Come here." He pulled her toward him and rested her head on his shoulder. "I'm just happy it worked." Then he whispered in her ear. "So this is our secret, right?"

She nodded.

"When you meet Mrs. Roosevelt, never mention this. OK?"

She looked up. "Don't worry, Jack."

They sat on the bench holding hands for another 15 minutes, filling the time with small talk and smiles. Tourists drifted in and out of the rock garden, paying little attention to the young couple in love. But their presence seemed to agitate Jack. He fidgeted on the bench. Emma sensed that he was waiting for the right time to say something. He mentioned his Chicago trips as if to open the door for her. He didn't discuss his activities; they were his private domain, off-limits to everyone outside the Roosevelts, including her. Now the door was being opened. She wondered why.

"My most recent trip to Chicago was significant," he said.

She said nothing. She could tell Jack wanted to jump over the conversational creek, but he hesitated.

"You know I normally don't discuss my work."

"Jack, you never discuss your work. That's OK with me. I understand. But, if you have a problem, I'm here. If you can't trust me with your world, who can you trust?"

He smiled. "It's not just a matter of trust, Emma. I need your help. And I need all your help. Ethan, Zak, and even your uncle."

She was intrigued now. "What could our little group possibly offer you?"

He thought for a moment. "I'm stuck between a rock and a hard place. I can't go to anyone else for help. No one. But I've been entrusted with a critical task. I must maintain the safety of Mr. Roosevelt." He looked around as if the birds were taking notes. "For the moment, I will only tell you that sometime in the coming week, someone will attempt to kill the Mayor of Chicago. There is a strong possibility that Franklin Roosevelt will be near the action. I have been assured that no harm will come to him. But I can't just stand by and hope for the best."

Emma looked at Jack. He bore a look that went beyond concern. He could hardly get the words out. She made sure she wore a look of shock when she heard this news. "But Jack, why not just tell the police? Tell the Secret Service. They could stop it. Tell Mrs. Roosevelt. She could make Mr. Roosevelt cancel his visit. If you have inside information, you could put an end to this right now. I don't get it."

Jack tried to speak. But he was so frustrated that he just stumbled over his words. "That's just it, I can't tell anyone, and I can't stop them."

"Why not?"

"It's complicated," he said. And then he thought for a moment. "No, it's not complicated. We are dealing with dangerous and powerful people. These are men who are used to getting their way. They have little regard for human lives other than their own. From their point of view, Miami, at this moment, is the perfect time and place to fix a problem once and forever. They may do the deed before Roosevelt comes to town, or they may not. But they will act."

"Does Mr. Roosevelt know about this?"

"I don't really know, but I would say not."

"And Mrs. Roosevelt?"

"I can't say. I know that Mayor Cermak is coming here to see Mr. Roosevelt. That meeting will assure the mayor will be out in the open, exposed to danger."

"But why does it have to happen?"

Jack made a face. "Because that's the way things are, Emma. It's not a pleasant world. Politics, in its broadest sense, is a messy business. There are no knights in shining armor."

"Not even Mr. Roosevelt?"

"No. FDR is a politician. And a damned good one. No doubt he knows Mayor Cermak has endangered his own life. The police know about the threats," he shook his head, "but Roosevelt doesn't know the specifics. And he should never know them."

"Why not?"

"If he did, he might be expected to act on such information. But that would not be in his or our best interests. He must remain above all this dangerous but ultimately petty activity. He will soon be the President of the United States, guiding the fate of millions of people."

"You mean no one is willing to stop this tragedy from happening?"

"I don't know. And I don't know if it is a tragedy. This whole thing is all about a Chicago gangland turf war. Something that doesn't involve us. In any event, it makes no difference. I am in it now. I know too much, but I can't tell anyone except you. And I'm coming to you for help. Because now I am responsible."

"What can we do? We're not police," she said. Then she stopped talking. She realized this was the opportunity they needed if they were to have a chance to save FDR. Jack knew that danger was a menacing cloud soon darkening this sunny Florida paradise. FDR was in peril. His station in life required him to move steadily and surely, like a man of super-confidence, without a care in the world, seemingly oblivious to the dangers around him, and little could be done. Even though she had no knowledge of politics, she suspected that events in this arena often made no sense to outsiders. And she also knew that without an intervention of some sort, FDR would die next week. Strangely, Jack was part of their team now. It didn't matter that he thought he was driving the mission. They all had the same goal.

"I'm sorry," she said. I'm acting like a little girl. Of course, we will help. Whatever we can do, we'll do it."

"Emma. You're the best." He kissed her and smiled. "Let's go."

-Chapter XIII-

The Confluence

Outside, seated in the hotel patio area, the time travelers and Jack Travers drank iced tea and planned the future. The noise from hotel guests swimming in the nearby pool provided cover for their conversation. Under the palm trees, Travers explained the limitations of their involvement in the coming action. Ethan thought this was the break they needed, somebody on the inside to help them stop the assassination. He had dozens of questions, and Jack answered many of them. But the central question they had was a simple one. Why not cancel FDR's visit to Miami? They thought of many excuses that would work, but Jack was adamant. The answer was no. There would be no interruption of FDR's schedule. If there was an interruption, there would be questions and inquiries. Thousands of people in Miami would be disappointed. The mobster war in Chicago could turn even uglier. And Jack hinted that Mayor Cermak was just a little bit too independent. In his opinion, Anton Cermak ran Chicago politics outside the boundaries of the national party leaders. What the country needed now was solidarity. Everyone should rally around Mr. Roosevelt and let him use his powers and influence to set the country back on track.

"But, it would be so simple to remove FDR from the danger zone," said Ethan.

"The most direct route is not always the most sensible," said Jack. "We have no choice in this matter."

"Can we get more information? We need something to go on. Someplace to start. What about looking into the Italian community here in Miami? It's not too much of a stretch to assume the Italian mobsters would work within their world." Ethan would have liked to tell Jack that all they had to do was find Giuseppe Zangara, and the pieces to the puzzle would come together, but that knowledge could not be shared. In fact, he had already looked through the local telephone directory hoping that the future assassin would have a phone. But this was 1933, and phones were a luxury. It would not be that simple.

"Not a bad idea, Ethan. The only name I have is Dave Yaras, which doesn't sound Italian to me. Nitti told me Yaras would be watching me. They might be watching us right now; the bellboy, bartender, or doorman might be one of his people. We must be careful. Yaras is the guy in charge. I've checked him out. He's a bad guy." He paused. "What's new? I don't think we want to mess with him. And if you're looking for a Little Italy in this town, you won't find it. There is none. Immigrants from Italy are few and dispersed. Despite the promises of the real estate developers, the gondolas, the Venice of America, the Italianate architecture, you won't find many Italians here."

"What about staying close to Mayor Cermak? After all, he is the target," asked Currant.

"I hate to put it this way, A.C., but unless Cermak is near FDR, it's none of our business." Jack sipped his tea. "We can't be responsible for his well-being. Anyway, I rode the same train with him coming down from Chicago. I can assure you he has a well-trained crew of guards with him. I also know he wears a bulletproof vest while in public. Roosevelt also has his protection with him at all times. So, none of us should make any fast moves near these men. The word is out. The Secret Service and the mayor's bodyguards are both on edge. I'm asking you to help me get Franklin Roosevelt safely onto the train back to New York. I'm not asking you to take a bullet. We need to anticipate, watch, and wait. I don't know exactly what will happen. Nor where. I only know something is about to happen. If we can do that, we will have done our job."

Travers pulled out a pack of cigarettes. "Does that

make sense to you?" He lit a cigarette and took a deep drag while waiting for a response.

Ethan looked at Zak. "Any ideas, *amigo*? You feeling anything?"

Zak thought for a moment.

"You know, Jack, that Zak is our resident intuitive," said Ethan. "Seriously, he has a sixth sense."

Jack nodded. "Emma told me about Zak. And I know something about seers. Like Edgar Cayce. They brought him in to help solve the Lindbergh baby kidnapping last year. I'm not saying I'm not a believer, but I am more of a nuts and bolts guy.

Zak listened to the discussion and impatiently tapped his fingers on the metal tabletop.

"Wait, I think The Great Zak is about to speak," said Ethan.

"Thank you for the wonderful intro," signed Zak.

Emma started to translate for Jack and A.C. Currant's benefit.

"No need, Emma. I understand. I think I can follow Zak's words," said Travers.

"You understand?" Emma was surprised.

"Something I picked up in England," he said flatly without additional explanation.

"I am certain Mr. Roosevelt is in mortal danger unless we act quickly and decisively."

"Thanks, Zak, short and to the point," said Travers. "Your crystal ball only reinforces my concern."

Zak pushed. *"Cermak will die, and so will FDR."*

Travers understood. "I appreciate your thoughts, but remember that's not the deal I made, Zak. It's up to us to see that nothing like that happens."

Zak just nodded. Ethan saw that he was frustrated with Travers's overconfidence.

A.C. Currant placed his empty glass on the table, leaned back, and spoke confidently. "Jack, I don't want to steal your thunder, but I have an idea."

"Don't worry about me. That's why I got you involved."

"OK. We're looking for a needle in a haystack. Why don't we become a magnet?"

"A.C., please," said Emma, "no riddles."

"Right, my dear. I'm suggesting that we go inside their world and make it known that we are looking for trouble. I think trouble will come to us and save us time and shoe leather."

"Where's that?" asked Ethan.

"I'd start with the dog track," said Currant. "Specifically, the Miami Beach Kennel Club. A place where people place bets on dog races. And as I remember, it's reputed to have some connection to Al Capone. And Al Capone ties right into Frank Nitti. And Frank Nitti to our current dilemma."

Jack Travers smiled. "That makes sense, A.C. Anyway, it's a good place to start. Dollars to donuts that place is mobbed up."

"Yes. And I wouldn't mind laying down a few bets on the pooches," said Currant.

Zak looked at him and signed. *Do you know anything about dog racing?* Currant looked to Emma for help.

Emma translated, and Currant responded. "Nope. Just sounds like fun to me."

"One more thing," said Jack. "I won't be with you. I can't. I have to maintain a measure of deniability. The Roosevelts cannot appear to have any involvement or knowledge of the terrible thing that may happen soon. You people are an unknown quantity. But they'll be watching me. So I'm asking you to help, knowing that you must be cautious and that I will be on the sidelines. You may be rubbing shoulders with some pretty undesirable characters. I'm serious. If you take this on, you must be careful."

"Jack," said Currant, "you forget that some of us have experienced life." He jutted out his chin as he spoke. "I saw some action with your boss's uncle back in '98. The Rough Riders. You may have heard of them." Currant straightened up as if called to attention.

Travers looked surprised.

Ethan was surprised. He looked at Currant and rolled his eyes.

"Didn't know that," said Travers. "How exciting. You were with Teddy Roosevelt in Cuba?"

The old inventor retreated. "Well, no. I was with the boys who got left behind in Tampa. A touch of the fever, you know. But we were right there on San Juan Hill...in spirit."

"That's good to know. I feel better asking all of you to fight the battle of Miami with you in the saddle."

"At your service, Jack. We'll do the job." He gave Travers a playful salute.

"Just remember. Your job is eyes and ears. No heroics. Don't approach any of these mobsters. If need be, leave that to me. We just have to find out what's really happening without making any waves."

The following day they didn't see Jack Travers. He and Emma had been out on the town the night before. Ethan was asleep by the time she returned to their room, but he stirred when she came in sometime after midnight. While waiting for breakfast to be served, Ethan studied his sister. She looked tired, and Ethan blamed it on her engagement with Jack.

Over coffee and Danish, they planned the day. For the morning, they would split up. Ethan and Emma would go to the dog track early, and Currant and Zak would mentally pretend they were assassins. As they had in Dallas five years earlier, they would check out the killing zone. They knew it would happen on February 15 at Bayfront Park. The announcement that FDR would be speaking hadn't made the local newspapers yet, but Jack had told them about it, and *The History* coldly spelled out the end result.

After breakfast, Currant and Zak headed across Biscayne Boulevard to the park, and the twins hailed a taxi. The driver made a quick U-turn, and soon they were on the Venetian Causeway, traveling from Miami to Miami Beach. A few minutes later, they were dropped off at the Kennel Club. The island at this southern point was narrow and offered a view across the bay of the downtown buildings of Miami. Nestled up against the ocean, the white stucco three-story Kennel Club building was impressive. A giant sign with six-foot-high letters that read *DOG TRACK* was on the roof.

"I guess they don't want anyone to miss it," said Ethan. The morning breezes off the ocean carried the scent of a tropical paradise. He remembered his recent adventure with Zak, fighting the blizzard and the drone dragonflies. He was glad to be in Miami.

Both he and Emma wore white. As they approached the building, he commented to her, "We really do look like twins today." He checked out her outfit. White cotton dress, a shell necklace, and rose-colored pumps. He wore a blue blazer, white pants, and a light blue open-collar shirt. His head was adorned with a Panama hat. They had done some shopping in the hotel boutique late yesterday afternoon. He grabbed her hand and paused as he glanced at his reflection in a shop window. "Check us out. We look pretty authentic."

She studied the reflections. "You know, brother, we're getting older. We look like adults now."

"Shocking," he said. "It happens. But at least I'm not getting married."

"Humph," she laughed. "Fat chance for you. But who knows? You clean up pretty well."

They crossed the street. The surf pounded into the pure white sandy beach a few hundred feet in front of them. Palm trees overhead, the dark blue Atlantic Ocean stretched to the horizon under a cloudless but misty sky.

They checked out the dog track as they walked along the waterfront access road. Beyond a wooden fence lay the oval track, which encircled a sea of grass with an island of flowers in the center. The grandstand looked like a giant rectangular clamshell on the other side of the raceway, thousands of seats sheltered by a curved cantilevered roof above. Next to it was a separate building.

"Looks good, eh?" he said.

"Let's go back and find a way in."

They found the front entrance and walked inside the cool, dark cavernous underbelly of the structure. A little man with a lobby broom and dustpan stopped his activity and approached them. "You need some help?" He had a foreign accent. "We not open for two more hours." Emma smiled at him. He looked up at her like she was an Amazon.

Emma held her leather portfolio in front of her in a clipboard fashion. Ethan carried a vest pocket camera in his hand. They were supposed to be reporters. "We work for the *Frederick News* in Frederick, Maryland. We're down here to do some human interest stories. We'd like to talk to some of your people if we could. You know, human interest stuff." She smiled again.

The man cut her short. "I no know. You talk to boss. Mr. Norris. He fix you up." He escorted them down the concourse.

Norris was not there, but his assistant, a clean-cut man in his late twenties, talked with them. Emma handed him a phony business card. He wore a yellow short-sleeve shirt with the name of the dog track embroidered on the vest pocket and his name, Vince, written above. She told the story again—just human interest, free publicity for the track—fun in the sun. He seemed disinterested. He told them his boss would not be in until later in the day. Emma threw a little more charm in his direction. Finally, he agreed they might be able to speak with some of the people on staff. He made a phone call, explained the situation to someone, and directed them to the adjacent building. "Talk to Martha. And see me again before you leave," he said. "Maybe Mr. Norris will be in by that time."

A short walk outside brought them to the annex building, an Italianate structure that belonged on a canal in Venice, not on a dog track in Miami Beach. It was impressive but phony. Fittingly, a fortyish buxom bleached blonde popped her head out of a door and waved them in. The woman wasn't too keen about having them interview her staff of dealers, waitresses, hat-check girls, cooks, and bartenders. Emma's charm would be wasted on this woman, thought Ethan. So, he applied some of his own. He explained that most folks back home had never been to Florida or the Kennel Club. "I know you're a VIP." He smiled. "But just give us a bit of your valuable time."

He convinced her to let him capture her photo outside with the grandstand in the background. He offered his arm, and they walked out to an open area. Dropping down on one knee to get a low-angle shot, he gave direction. "Tilt your head a bit." She offered her best side and sucked in her stomach. "Big smile now. Your eyes look beautiful." He snapped the photo even though there was no film in the camera. "I'll send you a copy of this as soon as it runs." He wrote down the woman's name and title in a little leather-covered notepad. "That's it, Martha. Thank you so much."

The woman released her stomach and beamed brightly. "Keep it down to a few minutes each, Ethan."

"Will do. Love those peepers, Martha." He smiled, and she headed back to her office.

She allowed them to quickly interview employees as they entered to start the day. Their goal: ask as few innocuous questions of as many employees as possible, tie a face with a name, and work the place later. In this way, they got to know them. Emma's interviewing skills came in handy. But they worked as a team, hoping to befriend everyone from the bartenders to the poker dealers. They got to know this part of the Kennel Club operation in less than half an hour of playful banter and seemingly innocent questioning.

Of all the people they talked to, one caught Ethan's attention. The good-looking hat-check girl named Angela said she would be working tonight. He made a show of noting this fact in his notepad. "See you tonight, Angela," he said with a smile. "I'm looking forward to it."

She also smiled. "I hope so," she replied in a soft voice.

On their way out, they returned to the building office. Norris was not back. They thanked Vince and promised to mail him a copy of the story before printing it; they also told him they would come back later to shoot some background photos of the races. He grunted, waved them out, and put his nose back into his paperwork.

Chapter XIV

A Day at the Races

Later that day, the time travelers arrived at the Miami Beach Kennel Club. Currant and Zak made the first race, and the twins showed up later. The pairs of spies would not associate with each other. They had separate missions. Currant was to adopt the look of a high roller accompanied by Zak as his apparent boy-toy. Although uncomfortable in his designated role, Zak went along with the program. In the cool shade of the grandstand box, the old man and the young man sat together admiring the view. The sepia-colored oval track surrounded a sea of green. Beyond lay the ocean, vibrating with shades of blue. The mass of people, vacationers, ordinary men and women, society guys and gals, and rails birds of all stripes and colors bubbled with excitement. Zak made a face when A.C. puffed his cigar and then released the smoke in his direction.

"*Must you?*" he begged in pained silence.

"Listen, my little friend," said Currant, "I'm just playing a part, and this Cuban is a prop. You should spend more time wearing an adoring look while simply admiring my presence and complaining less about cigar pollution."

Zak smiled and grudgingly pretended to be having a wonderful afternoon playing the rich man's fool.

Currant was familiar with dog racing, but he preferred the horses. He described today's venture as "going to the dogs." However, he didn't expect to increase his traveling money at the dog track. He planned to return to Hialeah in a couple of days to replenish his funds. He brought newspaper reprints of every race run for the 1932-1933 season, which made his horse betting technique unbeatable. Betting on the ponies, done with discretion, assured the time travelers a constant source of 1933 money. So much for fairness, he thought, knowing that things would even out today. Betting at a dog track in 1933 was for suckers. Nobody really knew what was going on with the dogs. They all looked the same to A.C. Currant. The greyhounds were just greyhounds except for their different colored jackets and the numbers imprinted on them. Inside information would help in the selection of winners. Currant was confident the owners, handlers, and track management had plenty of that commodity, but John Q. Public was, as usual, operating by the seat of his pants. They watched the dogs hustle around the oval track, feverishly chasing an elusive tin hare they could never catch. A.C. knew that his goal for the day was not to win but instead was a ploy to establish himself as a player, a mark, or a chump. He did a good job. Currant bet big on every race, losing every one of them.

Zak placed a few small wagers, and, not surprisingly, he won many of his races. He always claimed he could read animals. Later he told everyone that if anyone really understood the life of a racing dog, they wouldn't support the sport. The average racing dog's life was one of constant confinement and abuse. Overbreeding was the norm, and unwanted dogs were put to death, starved, or used for target practice. "*These dogs are miserable*," signed Zak.

Currant noticed Zak was losing focus. "Not our problem." He reminded Zak that they were there to tap into Frank Nitti's world, not the canine world.

As the day progressed, the shadow cast by the grandstand roof overhang slowly slid across the field, covering half of the oval. One more race would end the session. Still, it appeared that no one had fingered them. Currant placed a final bet of fifty dollars on a dog named Rough Rider to cement his image. Amazingly, the dog won the race and returned almost three hundred dollars. Zak and Currant left their box seats to claim their winnings. Amid the crowded corridor, A.C. flipped through his wad of bills, chewed on his cigar, and attempted to be as conspicuous as possible. He ceremoniously handed over a couple of twenties to Zak, who eagerly accepted them and reciprocated by giving his sugar-daddy a quick hug. This routine attracted a fair amount of attention from the ring of bettors around them, including some not-so-pleasant comments. But Currant was quite pleased with his performance. He tucked his newfound winnings into his wallet. Just then, a man approached. Dark-haired, thin, tall, and acne-faced, the visitor wore a fake smile and a large gold pin on his blazer bearing the name of the dog track.

"Congratulations, Mr...."

Currant looked at him curiously. "Doctor...Arthur C. Currant."

"Excuse me, doctor, for interrupting, but we here at the Kennel Club would like to invite you to enjoy the extended facilities of the club." He looked over at Zak. "And your friend also, of course."

"Well, Zak. We have made some new friends," said the smiling Currant. Returning his gaze to the man, he queried, "What exactly are you suggesting, sir?"

The man cued his auto-smile again. "We have a poker room for special guests. And all the drinks and food are complimentary."

Currant looked at his wristwatch. "I imagine we could find the time. I presume you're serving some giggle water." He smiled again.

"You won't be disappointed. Please...follow me."

Currant and Zak followed the man through the building to the adjacent annex building. Minutes later, standing in the second-floor reception area, they sipped champagne and noshed on *hors d'oeuvres*. The early evening sun was low in the sky; in the distance, the downtown buildings of Miami punctuated the skyline. The two men now were silhouetted against the window as the last rays of sunlight slid past them and filled the room with a rosy glow. Zak was the first to spot Ethan and Emma entering the room. He winked to get

Currant's attention and turned his head toward the door. Currant followed his lead, and his eyes connected with Ethan's. Ethan nudged his sister and looked in the direction of Zak and Currant. She also recognized them.

The twins moved toward the coat room. From across the room, the gambling duo watched. Angela, the hat-check girl, smiled when Ethan approached. She took his Panama hat, filed it on a shelf, and handed him a stub. It was a slow-motion transaction. She held it tight while he reached for it, a silly game of tug-of-war, thought Currant. She's just trying to get his attention.

Emma figured it out. She drifted away, moving to the bar. Ethan and the girl talked. They were too far away across a room full of loud, liquored-up people to pick up the conversation. The woman smiled and laughed. Ethan leaned into the opening. Something is going on, thought Currant. She was a good-looking woman: early twenties, wavy black hair, tan with bright white teeth, nicely put together, and wearing only a token coating of makeup. If he was thirty years younger, he would be interested. Obviously, young Ethan was.

Then Currant remembered her. She was the woman he had seen with Zangara on his first trip to 1933. Zak got Currant's attention. He mimed a warning to stop staring. Currant went back to his boy; the charade continued. When Currant and his protege for the poker room, Ethan continued to engage the brunette. And Emma was at the bar. She had already attracted the attention of a swarthy, slick-looking gent, and their conversation was flowing. Hopefully, it was sprinkled with helpful information.

A muscular man wearing a tuxedo guarded access to the card room. Zak and Currant walked confidently and paid little attention to the caretaker as if life in the fast lane was the norm. The raw-featured man gave them the once-over and then swung open the door. A blast of hot air and cigarette smoke wafted over them. Currant surveyed the space. Red carpet, gold-painted trim everywhere, green felt tabletops, and thick drapes covering the windows. It was a hot night. The building's rudimentary air conditioning system helped make the atmosphere tolerable, but the sweat, smoke, and noise were oppressive. Currant loosened his tie.

"This will be a long night, Zak. Keep out of trouble. And don't be coming on to some other guy. You're my boy."

Zak made a face. Currant could tell he was tiring. But the evening was just beginning.

Poker was a game that Currant remembered, but he had never played a crooked game. Most of his experience had been gained years ago when he was a college undergraduate playing against his blue-blooded brethren. In those days, he was a reasonably strong player with a consistent winning record. But that was then. He hadn't played a serious game in over fifty years.

The poker room had a dozen tables. They were all being played. Currant was seated at a table with five other players. Zak split off. A little later, Currant saw him, beer in hand, heading into an adjacent slot machine room. Currant suspected the one-armed bandits were illegal, as was the liquor, but obviously, that was of no concern to anyone. They called Miami "Little Chicago," and so it was.

A.C. Currant had a simple plan of action. He would play poker, lose money, drink, and chat it up. He hoped to make himself known. "Hello, everyone," he chirped to the other players and the dealer, "I'm Doc Currant. A pleasure to join you." The other players smiled, frowned, or ignored his greeting. A well-dressed couple in their late thirties, a little man with tinted glasses, a fat fellow who felt the need to wear a Panama hat indoors, and a dark-skinned, unpleasant-looking man made up the table. The latter, Currant guessed, was probably a house shill.

Currant had his game plan and stuck to it. He proved to be a good poker player, although anyone watching the game progress might not think so. He drank the bar scotch that was offered to him by roving waitresses. After playing a couple dozen hands, he appeared to be sliding into inebriation. This was not the case, A.C. Currant could hold his liquor, and the watered-down drinks were easily integrated. He managed his game to take several pots, but his winning hands would yield little, and his losing hands would lose big. All the while, he rewarded the dealer with excessive tips whenever he won. The time passed quickly. The couple had fun and shared pleasant banter with Currant; the little man hugged his chips and said nothing; the fat fellow was always unhappy and groused the entire time, and the shill won. The dealer appeared to be an old hand at this poker business and announced that he was done for the night. Another dealer immediately filled the gap.

Currant cashed in, and he caught up with the dealer as he walked away. "Hey, friend, are you available for a drink?"

The man, whose face revealed the struggles of his five decades of life and whose pickled nose showed his need for alcohol, looked back at Currant quizzically. Then he remembered him. "How's that?"

"Care for a drink? My friends seem to have left me. And I'm not one to drink alone."

While he ran his hand over his five-o'clock shadow, the dealer glanced at a well-dressed, slicked-down guy watching the tables, a management guy. Currant guessed the dealer was concerned about fraternizing with the suckers. But it didn't stop him from accepting A.C.'s invitation. "Why not? I could use a drink. It's been a long day, and I'm not gettin' any younger."

They sat at the bar. Currant was handling the bar bill, and Leonard, his newfound friend, was OK with that. They covered this and that in their conversations, mostly talking about the perils and problems of getting older. Leonard was a transplant from New York City. He had given up on the winters up north two years ago. The country was in an economic depression, but Miami was breaking out. Legal gambling was helping to rejuvenate the town. When the dog tracks became legal in Florida, he packed it in and drove south. He had the manual dexterity and brainpower to handle the cards, and he jumped in when the demand for talented workers was at its peak. While they talked, he drank his old-fashioned with gusto. "One more, if you don't mind. "You a snowbird, too?"

"No, I came down here for the sun. Like everyone else. Just here for the fun of it. But today, I came here looking for a friend of mine. A guy I knew in Jersey. Joe Zangara. I know he loves the dogs, so I thought I might run into him here. You ever see him? He's a little guy. Not an inch over five foot tall. Built like a stick. Italian. Heavy accent. I owe the guy." Currant downed his scotch. "You think I'd be running the other way, but that's me. If I don't pay my bills, I can't sleep. Does that happen to you?"

Leonard laughed. "Are you kiddin' me? I guess people are different. I don't hold grudges, think about unpaid bills, or worry about tomorrow. Ya' know?"

Currant laughed. "Ain't that the truth." He put one elbow on the bar and put his chin in his hand, pretending to be drunk. He just looked at the man for an uncomfortably long time. Finally, he spoke. "So, Leonard," his words slurred, "ever see old Joe around here?"

Leonard seemed to really be working his brain. Then he brightened. "Is this Joe guy a pain in the ass?"

"That's the guy. He did some work on my house. Knew his business." Currant shook his head. "But he's got a bad attitude. Anyway, he disappeared before I could make his last payment. His landlady said he left for Miami."

Leonard took a deep breath. "I think I know him. Tiny little guy. I seen him a couple of times up here. A few weeks ago, he was makin' a stink about something. Right near my table. He said nobody could do that to Joey Z. I don't know who the hell he thought he was, but management tossed him out without a second thought.

They don't allow trouble here. Usually, they bounce guys pretty hard. But they went easy on your friend. Maybe he's in with somebody. Ya won't find him in here again. But I seen him on the rail. Couple a times a week. He's always here for the first race. A regular. He's a friend of one of the girls. The hat-check broad. What's her name? Olivia or Angela. Somethin' like that. Don't know what that babe sees in him. 'Cept he's a Wop, and so's she. But," he shook his head, "what do I know?"

"Thanks, friend. I'll look for him if I have time." Currant quickly turned the conversation to other topics. He suggested the man have another drink, but Leonard didn't answer. Currant had been sliding in closer to the dealer. No doubt, A.C. Currant looked and sounded sloppy drunk. Leonard rested his free hand on the bar. Currant was in the middle of a story when he casually bounced his hand lightly off the top of Leonard's hand to make a point. This was enough for Leonard. He looked at his watch and begged off. "Nice meetin' ya, Doc. I gotta go. See you around."

Currant tipped his imaginary hat to him, and he downed the remainder of his drink, satisfied that he had purchased good information. Zak then popped back into his world. Currant paid the bill, and they called it a night.

LOG of Zak Newman
February 9, 1933 (local time): 23:12 (Day 8 of time travel)

Now that was one tough day. Once we got back to the hotel, we met with Ethan and Emma. A.C. Currant revealed he made some headway. He found out that Zangara is a regular at the dog track. For all we know, the little killer might have been there today. But tomorrow, I'm going back to the track. If he's there, I will become his shadow. A.C. gave me a photo he copied out of the history book story on FDR's killing. I don't think I'll have any problem recognizing him. This should be fun. We'll find out where he lives. Then we can keep an eye on him. Ethan and I will have the task of finding and trailing Mr. Z from now until next Wednesday. On the day of the assassination, we may both follow him. We don't want to lose him.

Tomorrow, I'll be on detective duty. Dr. Currant will be at Hialeah refilling the financial coffers. Emma's spending the day with Jack Travers. And Ethan may be meeting with the hat-check girl. Lucky him. She looked pretty hot to me. He claimed somehow his interest in the girl was related to our quest, but I don't think he knew anything about her supposed friendship with Zangara until Dr. Currant mentioned it tonight. In fact, Ethan admitted, she practically asked him out. I can believe that. He's not exactly the smoothest guy romantically. It's not that the girls aren't interested in him. He's just a little lost when it comes to women. It's hard to believe that a big guy like Ethan gets so nervous around the gals. But he does. In any event, she gave him her phone number, and he will call her tomorrow. He seemed pretty excited about the whole thing.

End 02-09-33

-Chapter XV-

The Date

Ethan wanted to orient himself before meeting Angela. He had the taxi drop him at Ocean Drive and 7th in Miami Beach. It was mid-morning, and the temperature was rising. Palm trees lined the boulevard. Beyond the continuous landscaped park on the other side of the street, the Atlantic was calm. Crisp little waves relentlessly rolled in, the endless energy coils rhythmically erupting and exhausting themselves on the white sands. Even at this early hour, scattered sunbathers, swimmers, and colorful umbrellas dotted the beach. There was no evidence of the powerful hurricanes almost destroying this area a few years ago; the replacement and growth of trees, flowers, and shrubs had healed those wounds. Miami Beach was back in business.

A light breeze slipped beneath his white linen jacket and cooled him while the tropical sea air and balmy temps excited his senses. Today, he wanted to lose himself in the pleasure of the moment. He was alone, twenty-two years old, unattached, thousands of miles and a hundred years from home. This was the moment to be free and independent. And so he savored it. He truly wanted to forget his mission and let go of his unshakable concern for the future. He turned away from the ocean and headed down 7th Street. The driver had said her address was a few blocks west, an area of smaller hotels, all very white, clean, and modern.

When he telephoned her earlier this morning, a hotel person answered. That woman had shouted to someone that the call was for Angela. In time, she got on the line, and he stammered. Eventually, he recovered control of his words, and they agreed to meet. Her voice was pure magic. Last night, at the casino, they had connected. He couldn't get her out of his mind. She was there in his thoughts when he went to bed and again when he awoke. He longed to see her. When he entered the lobby of the small apartment hotel, she was waiting for him. She sat in a white wicker chair, surrounded by tropical plants, bathed in sunlight that glistened off her dark hair and tanned body, revealing a vision of paradise to Ethan. She smiled openly. Ethan walked to her, and like something he had seen in old movies, he extended both hands to meet hers. They met as he bent over. Against all odds, he kissed her on the forehead. The warm fragrance of her perfumed hair seeped into his subconscious and excited him.

She looked up and smiled. "Is that the way they do it in Frederick?"

For a moment, he had no idea what she was talking about. Then he recovered. "That is...the traditional Frederick greeting," he laughed, "with a dash of tropical fever. I must apologize. I don't usually kiss a girl in the first minute."

"I'll take that as a compliment." She stood, grabbed his hand, and dragged him gently out of the building onto the sidewalk. "Today is my day off from the Kennel. They are letting me run loose. What's your pleasure?" she said innocently.

"I'm at your command. Can we walk someplace where we can talk?"

"Follow me, Ethan." She dashed ahead, beckoning him on.

A few quick steps brought him to her side.

They walked to a nearby park and then strolled aimlessly. They did talk. He told her about his fictitious world in the little town near Washington, D.C. He had visited the burg on his trip in 1932, so he could make the place dance with life as he regaled her with tales of chasing fire trucks, covering local flower shows, and taking photos of the mayor kissing babies. She talked about her life in Miami Beach. She lived with her father in the hotel. He ran a tiny tailor shop on the first floor that served the guests and the residents of the other nearby hotels. Her full name was Ottavia Angela Marra. In 1920, at the age of ten, she came to the United States from a small town in southern Italy. She spoke no English when she arrived. He joked with her, lamely suggesting he couldn't understand her. She recoiled as if wounded. He started to apologize but stopped when she laughed aloud. Her large, dark brown eyes smiled at him, providing dispensation. She, too, could joke, and he relaxed.

They walked hand in hand through the park. Ethan floated along, riding on the lilt of her voice, watching her shiny black hair swing to and fro and occasionally receiving a nudge from her body when she drifted into his path. She was as playful as a little girl. And slowly, he was finding he also could unwind. The sun, the ocean breeze, the quiet, luxurious tropical air, the cobalt blue sky, and the beautiful Italian girl walking with him released his inhibitions. This was all new to him, exciting, and strange in a good way.

They spent the morning together, had lunch at a diner, and then returned to her apartment building. She introduced her father, Salvatore, who was busy working in his tailor shop. Ethan found the small, half-bald, foreign-looking man of gentle disposition exceptionally courteous. He made up for his limited capacity to speak English by smiling and gesturing to excess. Angela hugged him.

"Papa, we are going to have a glass of lemonade upstairs. And then I will come down and help you. All right?"

"*Bene. Bene*," he said. "You go. No *problema*." He smiled at Ethan, and they shook hands. Then he went back to sit at his old-fashioned sewing machine. It was whirring as they left.

Angela and her father lived on the second floor of the apartment hotel. Ethan entered, and the space quickly made itself known: a Pullman kitchen with a dropped countertop for dining that separated a scattering of furniture in the living room. A pair of half-shuttered windows capped the end. Sunlight made its way in, but the view was limited to the white stucco wall of the light well. A small bedroom and bathroom completed the apartment. He thought it a little too cozy, but he tried not to show any discomfort. She turned on the radio and found a station playing music.

"Sit," she said from the other side of the counter.

He removed his jacket, folded it, laid it on the arm of the sofa, and sat down.

"I'll get something to drink."

While Angela retrieved a pitcher of lemonade from the refrigerator, Ethan stared at the white box with the strange metal doughnut on top. He was fascinated with the ancient appliance. It was a museum exhibit for him. Angela was to be a joy to watch as she moved about. He had crazy thoughts of intimacy with this woman he had met only yesterday. They were the typical thoughts of a man his age but new to him. He was alone with a beautiful girl in a strange world. This apartment was a tiny stage waiting for a love scene to be played out with a woman who was long dead in his time. He was simultaneously living in the moment and observing himself. It was all very confusing.

"Here you go. I made it fresh today. One thing we have here is plenty of lemons." She chuckled. She returned, set the small tray holding two glasses and a pitcher on the coffee table, and then sat next to him. She poured; they raised their drinks high and clinked. "*Buona fortuna.*"

They both smiled, sipped, and gazed at each other. Then setting the drinks on the table and adding one more look for confirmation, they embraced. This moment was over the top for Ethan. The woman he held close was only a year older than him, but she was certainly more experienced than he in the art of loving. Quickly their coupling became all-consuming for him. He felt the heat of her body. He was reaching for more intimacy than she had anticipated. She pushed him away. They both took in deep breaths.

"I'm sorry," he said. "I don't know what came over me."

She smiled and sipped her lemonade. "Oh, I think I have the idea, Ethan. It's been a while, hasn't it?"

He didn't know how to answer that question without sounding stupid and inexperienced, so he nodded.

"This is not a good place or time," she said slowly. "This whole thing is so crazy."

"Right. Crazy. You said it." His face was flushed, and suddenly, he felt very awkward.

"Maybe you like me because you are far away from home. Far away from your girlfriend," she said tauntingly.

"No...that's not it." He shook his head. "I don't have a girlfriend."

She snapped her head back in mock disbelief. "You don't have a girl. A good-looking gentleman like you. Shame on you. You're not...?"

"What?"

"You know. You don't...ah...prefer boys to girls. Do you?"

He laughed. "Now you're playing with me, aren't you?"

She nodded and laid her head on his shoulder. "*Un poco.*"

He reached down and lifted her chin gently to look into her eyes. "I heard you have a boyfriend. I would think you have many. You're so beautiful."

"Who is telling you that?"

"Somebody at the club told a friend of mine. He said you spent your free time with a man at the dog track. A little guy. Older. Is that true?"

She made a face and sat quietly for a moment as if offended. "Who, Giuseppe Zangara? He's not my boyfriend. He's a cousin of mine. From Italy. He's a hopeless case. A drifter. A lot of problems. Owes some money to some bad people. He's on a losing streak at the track. And his stomach always hurts. He's a wreck. My father wants me to help him by listening to him complain and by being sympathetic." She leaned back. "You think that he would be my boyfriend?"

"I hope not," he said abruptly. He was startled by the name "Zangara," the guy they were trying to find and stop before he killed Franklin Roosevelt.

"Why not?"

He thought for a moment. "I'm not the kind of guy who pushes his way into a relationship. And..."

"And what, Mr. Ethan?"

"And I like you. I like you a lot."

"I like you too." She smiled. "But we can't stay here any longer. People will start to talk. And I have to help papa. Drink your lemonade, and we go. OK?"

Ethan had no argument. But he did kiss her again. If this was it, he wanted to make the best of it. Their kiss was about to expand, but she broke it off again. "You are a bad boy," she said. "I will tell my papa about you." She smiled again brightly. He let the image of this beautiful woman sink into his memory.

Then quickly, as if they were about to be discovered, they cleaned up and left. Ethan didn't see her father on the way out. In the lobby, they said goodbye with a hug. She hoped to see him soon. He quickly kissed her again, and they parted. As he walked away, he felt alive and happy.

Early afternoon Ethan returned to his hotel. Everyone was out. He waited, but with nothing to do, he contemplated a swim in the pool. After donning his swimming trunks and robe and walking outside, he found a towel and lounge chair and surveyed the pool. Surprisingly, only a few people were soaking themselves, and no kids were swimming. He tossed his robe on a chair, stood near the pool at the edge of the deep end, and executed a clean plunge dive.

Ethan was a good athlete at a time in his world when athleticism was on the decline. Soon, he rolled over and floated on his back. His legs spread-eagled and arms floating above his head, he relaxed into a semi-stupor. Eyes closed, the sun beat down on him. Occasionally, he would pop them open, becoming aware of the world again. A palm tree border ringed a blue sky rectangle; seagulls drifted above. His eyes closed again; he was at peace.

He thought about Angela. She was the first girl who had ever made such a connection with every part of his being. He had spent time with girls before and even fully physically connected with one, but there was no magic about them. But there was magic when he thought of Angela. How unfortunate, he ruminated. He had found the girl of his dreams, but she lived in another time. Then he thought about Emma. She had the same problem. Now he realized he hadn't focused on the obvious—that falling in love was uncontrollable, unforeseeable, and undeniable. In the pool with the water lapping gently at his body, for the first time, he understood his sister's dilemma and the immensity of her decision to return home. She was in love with Jack Travers. It made no difference that they were two people of different times. That was a fact of life for both of them. He was utterly lost in his thoughts when he heard a voice calling him. The water in his ears made the sound tinny, but he knew it was the voice of Jack Travers. He opened his eyes and lifted his head. Jack's head was silhouetted in the sun.

"Come on out, Ethan. Let's talk."

Ethan folded up, swam to the edge, and bounded out onto the deck like a seal. Travers moved back quickly to avoid the shower of water.

They sat near the pool, facing each other in lounge chairs. "Glad I caught you without the others. "Where's Emma?"

"She's resting in your room," said Jack. "We had a swell day. We saw a movie. *Scarface* with Paul Muni. It's all about the Italian mob against the Irish mob. I'll save you the trouble...the Italians win. Anyway, I saw your clothes lying on the bed, and I figured you went for a dip. So here I am. Productive day for you? Or at least fun?"

Ethan ran one hand across the back of his head. "Both," he said. "Angela and I really hit it off. Did Emma talk about her?"

Travers nodded. "She said she's a looker. But she also said she may already have a boyfriend. According to A.C., Angela spends many of her afternoons at the track with him."

"Not a boyfriend. A cousin. A guy named Zangara."

"They're related?"

Ethan wished he could tell Travers the truth about Zangara, but that was impossible. "That's what she said. She didn't go into details, but I get the idea he has a lot of personal issues. Owes the wrong people money. And health issues. She just babysits him to make her father happy."

"OK. Good for you, Valentino." Travers laughed.

"Let's put it this way. I wouldn't mind seeing her again."

"No problem. Anyway, I wanted to talk to you about Emma."

Ethan relaxed. He swung back into the chaise lounge and lay back. The sun was in his eyes. "Can I borrow your sunglasses?"

Travers dug them out of his jacket pocket and handed them over.

Ethan slipped them on. "Much better. What's up?"

"I'll be square with you." He straightened up. "I'm concerned. You don't like that Emma and I are involved. Is that a fact?"

Ethan thought for a moment. "You're right. It was an issue for me. Emma and I are twins, and so in a way, we have a special connection. And we've gone through a whole lot together. So I was thrown for a loop when she told me you two were engaged." He shrugged his shoulders. "Getting married. That's something. But today, I thought that regardless of my relationship with her, you two also have a special relationship. So special that my sister, who is impossible to please, has made a commitment to you."

"That's true. We are committed," said Jack.

"Well, I say, go for it."

Travers smiled. "That's a big load off my shoulders. Thanks. What about your father? And your uncle?"

"I wouldn't worry about A.C. He may act old-fashioned, but he's very modern. As far as Dad's concerned. He'll be shocked at the news, but in the end, he wants what's best for her. Is that you, Jack?"

"Yes," he said, without a moment's hesitation. "I love Emma. I'll protect her and do anything to make her happy."

Ethan took a deep breath and exhaled. "So that's that, future brother-in-law." Ethan laughed softly, knowing this impossible dream would never happen.

-Chapter XVI-

Man to Man

Over the weekend, Ethan and Zak had been successful in trailing Zangara. The direction from Travers had been simple: gather information and avoid trouble. On that level, they were successful, but as Currant reminded them, they had traveled to 1933 to save FDR. Jack Travers couldn't foresee the future. He might think he had everything under control, but the historical facts screamed otherwise. Somehow Giuseppe Zangara ended up killing FDR. Currant could not be sure whether intentional or accidental, but he was confident that FDR would die, that John Nance Garner would replace him on inauguration day, and that the world would never be the same.

Currant was disappointed in Ethan; it seemed like he had lost his focus. Before they left Mystic Heights, Ethan was a man possessed with the idea of saving FDR. But now, his mind was stuck in another groove. Angela had felled the giant with a tiny pebble of passion.

Currant was not unsympathetic. With some pain, he still remembered his first encounter with love. In 1972, he was a senior in high school, she was a cheerleader, and he was a nerd. They had been an unlikely couple. But she was not a dumb blonde, and he was not only a geek. She laughed at all his stupid jokes and marveled at his inventiveness. He admired her ability to solve crossword puzzles, her love for life, and everything about her physical person.

Looking back at their relationship, it was a fantasy. Two young people search for true love and discover each other's bodies. There were no rules for such discoveries, but in Currant's youth, young love remained young. He disliked generalizations, but in his view, the young people of 2033 were much more intelligent than the average young person of the 1970s. Still, they were far more gullible and emotionally immature. Emma probably was an exception. But Ethan was a perfect example of a young man lost in love—someone losing his grip on reality and drifting into a make-believe world.

Young love was not Currant's problem. Unlike Ethan, the cold reality of life was tightening its grip on him. A.C. Currant realized that he might live another fifty years. No one really knew the ultimate effects of the life-extension programs developed for highly-skilled intellectuals like him. As he contemplated having to live another half-century as a well-paid slave of the system, he began to consider decades more existence in a world where each day was duller than the previous. It was a slow, boring train going nowhere.

The *TimeTravelle* was his only relief. He used the machine recreationally to relate again to people with purpose. People who lusted for life. To others, these way-back places in time might, by today's standards, appear as crude and primitive as the Victorian era, but to Currant, they tasted delicious. But his visits would have to end. Every time he ventured out, he increased the possibility of being discovered. Time cops were real, and their only job was eliminating rogue travelers. He knew the end was coming.

That drove him to go on this trip with his young friends. That was why he hoped Franklin Delano Roosevelt would live to be considered the greatest president in the history of America—the man who saved the passenger-citizens of the American sinking ship of state. Of course, he couldn't be sure of Roosevelt's potential effect, but it wasn't just the enthusiasm of Ethan, Emma, and Zak that caused him to change his mind. Instead, it was his own careful analysis of the man. In his mind and heart, FDR was the only possible person who could save the people of 1933 and the future of the United States. Currant now was totally invested in this venture to save the man. FDR had to live; A.C.

Currant was now determined to impact history.

At the Miami Beach dog track, the aging time-traveler searched for the person who held the nation's fate in his hands, the thirty-two-year-old, one hundred-five-pound Italian immigrant Giuseppe Zangara. In the future world, Currant had viewed the old newsreels of the proclaimed assassin. He appeared amazingly calm and happy in his jail cell, awaiting execution. He seemed to be enjoying his notoriety without any fear of death. He joked with his jailer. Clean-cut, quick-witted, and always smiling, he almost made light of his motive for the crime: a supposed need to rid the world of kings and presidents. Like an actor following a script, he would say, "My stomach always hurt, so I killed the president."

Later reports would describe him as sullen, but this was not evident in the interviews. Zangara seemed to be a man who had been up against the wall, but once in jail, he recognized the freedom that death would bring. His last words before he was executed were: "*Viva Italia! Viva Camorra!* Good-bye to the poor people everywhere." Then, when nothing happened, he said: "Pusha da button. Go ahead and pusha da button." They did, and he died quickly. Facing death, Zangara could have said anything. But he felt the need to say, "*Viva Camorra!*" Currant knew that the Camorra, a collection of Neapolitan crime clans, was Italy's oldest and largest crime organization. The news media in 1933 seemed to have little interest in Zangara's apparent connection to the mob. To them, he was just another lone nut.

A.C. Currant scanned the dog track for the mysterious Zangara. He found the hapless little man leaning on the rail, loudly berating a hound that came in second place.

"*Porco cane! Porco miseria!*" Giuseppe Zangara threw his program at the ground.

"*AND THE WINNER IS NUMBER 4...OEDIPUS REX....*" The track announcer then listed the race results and thanked the crowd for their attendance.

"So, you didn't have the tragic hero?" Currant spoke

as he sidled up to Zangara.

The man looked at Currant, and a frown filled his reddened face. He shook his head. "What?"

"These dogs will disappoint you. I had nothing but losers today. But tomorrow's another day. Right?"

Even though A.C. Currant spoke slowly and distinctly, Zangara appeared to be mechanically processing every word of a non-native language.

"Yeah. Tomorrow. No tomorrow." The sun caught his eyes, and he squinted to better look at Currant. "What do you want? I no know you."

Currant smiled. "But I know you. You're Giuseppe Zangara. You call yourself Joe. Should I call you Joe?"

"I...you no call me anything." He seemed startled by Currant's aggressive approach.

"Take it easy, Joe. I'm here to help you."

"Who are you?"

"I'm a guy who can take away all your worries."

Zangara scoffed. "Me. I got no worries. Who you work for?"

"I don't work for Dave Yaras. And I am not a cop. I'm a friend who thinks you could use a friend. Am I right?"

The man just looked at him. "You crazy. They say Joe is crazy. But you crazy. I no talk to you anymore. Leave me alone." He started to walk away.

"Joe. Wait. I know what you've been ordered to do. But you don't have to. I can help." Zangara stopped and looked back. Currant thought he made some slight connection. He moved closer to him. "Let's go for a walk. On the pier. No one can hear us there, and we can see if anyone is spying. Just give me five minutes, and I'll explain everything. OK?" He opened his wallet and pulled out a twenty-dollar bill, which he handed to the man. "Here, take this as my gesture of good faith."

Zangara grabbed the bill and quickly stuffed it into his pants.

Currant reached out to shake his hand. "I'm Doctor Currant." The man shook it. Currant was surprised at the size of Zangara's tiny, delicate hand. Then Currant lightly guided the man by the elbow and directed him toward the exit.

They walked on the ocean side of the dog track and followed the path leading to a concrete pier extending from the shore. A strong wind was blowing in off the Atlantic, and waves pounded the concrete pillars of the dock. Heavy clouds darkened the horizon. A few people milled about, but it wasn't a pleasant environment for sightseeing. Currant and Zangara turned their backs to the wind and leaned against the railing. Zangara had a compact rectangular head with a high brow, a prominent chin, and neat, symmetrical features. His skin was clean and dark, and his eyes black and deep. He had the hands of a young girl and the frame of a boy. He didn't look like a killer. They waited until the other people around them were tired from fighting the wind and headed back to shore.

Apparently satisfied they were alone, Joe Zangara spoke loudly above the noise of the pounding surf. "So, Doctor. Talk."

"You've got yourself into some trouble. Right?"

Joe Zangara nodded. "Uh-huh."

"Do you owe them money?"

"I owe lots of money."

"And you can't repay them?'

"No. I have no money."

"And what have they offered you? Did they tell you they will let you go free if you do the job for them?"

Zangara looked nervous. His eyes darted about as he looked over his shoulder down the pier as if their voices might be heard. "How you help me?"

"Look, Joe. I don't want you to shoot anyone. Are you supposed to shoot somebody?"

His eyes rolled. He didn't answer.

"Are you doing this because you owe them?"

"What do you do for me?"

"I can get you all the money you need to repay them what you owe."

"Why you give money to me?"

"Because I don't want to see anyone hurt. That's all. Will that fix it for you?"

He held his hand on his chin and reflected. "I no think so."

"Why not?"

"Because I took their money. I use it at horses. Dogs. I lose it all."

"They didn't loan it to you?"

"No."

"So you stole it?"

He pursed his lips. "Yes."

"Do you think they would take it if I give you enough money?"

He thought. "No. It no matter."

"What will happen if you don't shoot at the man?"

He answered quickly. "They kill everyone. My family in Italy, and America. And they kill me." He smiled. "I do what I am told. I not afraid. You give me money. I buy myself some ice cream."

At first, Currant didn't understand, but he pulled out his wallet and handed the man another twenty.

Zangara took the bill and added it to his collection. "You good man, Doctor. But I go now. You leave me alone. Or we both get more trouble."

"One thing, Joe. It's the mayor, right?"

He looked at Currant incredulously. His eyes narrowed. "Who ya think?"

"When will it happen?"

He shrugged his shoulders and extended his palms. Then he turned, walked up the pier, and disappeared into the nearby park.

Currant faced the ocean. The angry seas were rife with crosscurrents, and the wind blew with fury. He understood where Zangara stood. He had crossed the line, and he could never come back. Currant didn't know how the man got his hands on the mob's money, but he was a dead man once he took it. But even death was not sufficient to motivate a patsy like Joe Zangara. The resolute little man appeared to have the strength to suffer the consequences of his actions. He knew how things worked in Italy. It was no different here. Even in death, you were not free. They could make you pay even after you die. Zangara had no choice. He had to move ahead.

A.C. had taken the risk to make the overture. He knew Yaras's spies might have seen him, but it was worth the risk. Negotiation was always better than war. But this was now a dead end. Unless someone was willing to interfere with the plot, Zangara would make his attempt on Mayor Cermak. He was convinced Zangara had only one job to do, and that was to kill the mayor.

Emma's fiancé was clever. He had negotiated with the mob, and they struck a deal. But in the heat of battle, many things could go wrong. Friendly fire kills just as surely as that shot by the enemy. Currant was concerned the time travelers would become spectators again. In 1963 in Dallas, he had watched another president die at the hands of assassins. He had accepted that defeat. But he did not want to see that happen again. This time he would make sure.

He spoke briefly with Ethan and Zak when he returned to the hotel. He told them of his failed attempt to buy off the assassin. Zangara was going to complete his mission. Currant was also certain Jack Travers would do nothing to stop Zangara. Travers was probably hoping that Zangara would have an opportunity to kill Cermak before FDR arrived on the scene. This would be the best outcome for Jack Travers. FDR would be in the clear. There would be no interference with the Outfit, and life would go on, except for Mayor Cermak. But *The History* told another tale.

It was Ethan who suggested another approach.

"What about Angela? She's Zangara's cousin and friend. Maybe she would help us...somehow."

"It's worth a try, Ethan," said Currant.

"I won't see her again until tomorrow night. I hope it's not too late. But I don't want anything to happen to her.

We can't put her in danger."

"That's in your hands, Ethan. Be careful. But don't be timid," said Currant. "Maybe she can talk him into leaving town. Or maybe she can delay him until FDR is out of range."

LOG of Zak Newman
February 13, 1933 (local time): 22:15 (Day 12 of time travel)

After meeting with A.C. earlier, Ethan and I went to his room and talked. Ever since he met his friend Angela, his thinking has been mushy. I went for the jugular/a slap in the face/a splash of cold water. I wanted to be sure about him. Was he ready to do whatever it took to stop the assassination—including taking Zangara out of the equation early? Currant, Ethan, and I had discussed this as the only viable approach. It might be a gamble to interfere with the Outfit. But would it really be that bad? Assuming we just delay the little guy 15 or 20 minutes, Roosevelt will be safe.

According to The History, FDR is scheduled to arrive in Miami from his fishing trip on Wednesday the 15th. Late evening, he will make the short trip from the dock to Bayfront Park across the street from our hotel. His car will drive up on the road in front of the stage and park. FDR will make a short speech, sit for a couple of photos, and drive off into the sunset. Chicago's Mayor Cermak will be sitting up on the stage with a crowd of other dignitaries. When everyone begins to disburse after FDR leaves, there will be plenty of confusion and people milling about. Zangara will still be able to get close and do what he has to do. In fact, if Jack Travers is right, the Outfit would have no reason not to wait until Roosevelt leaves. FDR would be safe for certain. He and his crowd of bodyguards would be headed to the railway station. Thus, they would stick by their agreement and still get the job done.

The History says that Zangara shot and killed FDR, but we know the man only intends to kill Mayor Cermak. He will still have his opportunity. In fact, he may even have a better chance. All four of us have discussed the issue of allowing the attempt on the mayor to happen. None of us want anyone to get hurt, and we understand Jack's hands-off position. Sometimes the simplest solution is the best. If Zangara and Cermak make it to Bayfront Park two nights from now, we will keep Zangara from getting anywhere near the roadway on which Franklin Roosevelt will travel until Roosevelt is out of harm's way.

Ethan told me he is willing to do what it takes. He agrees with our plan. He's supposed to meet with Angela tomorrow night. He says he'll talk to her about her cousin—ask her to help. Zangara is a man caught in a vice. He will make his attempt on the 15th at Bayfront Park. We must find a way to manage him. As strange as it seems, this is all we can do. We really don't know what will happen, except that we are determined to keep FDR alive.

End 02-13-33

-Chapter XVII-

Round Two

February 14, 1933, St. Valentine's Day, Jack Travers was getting ready to meet with Emma. At this moment, he was a forgetful lover without a gift. His mind wandered through the possibilities. Each one seemed more predictable than the next. Emma would expect more from him than a bouquet or a box of chocolates. He pondered what St. Valentine might have given. Then he remembered that the saintly ringmaster of love had his head chopped off as a matchmaker in ancient Rome. Too much to give, he thought. Four years ago, on Valentine's Day, Al Capone's boys did a little chopping of their own when they machine-gunned seven members of the rival Bugs Moran gang—ahh, the romance of it all. In desperation. Jack had asked the hotel desk clerk for some creative ideas. The man suggested an evening listening to the new singing sensation Roberta Sherwood, who was performing at a nearby speakeasy. The desk clerk would secure the tickets and send them to Jack's room. Everything looked promising for a romantic night on the town.

As he dried himself with an oversized bath towel, his thoughts went back to the business of saving FDR. Tomorrow, Roosevelt would return from his fishing trip and make his speech in the park. Unfortunately, as far as Jack knew, Mayor Cermak was still alive. The newspaper reports had him visiting local dignitaries. He was maintaining a low profile. One day Zak visited Cermak's hotel and managed to get a glimpse of the mayor as he entered a cab. According to Zak, the man looked ill. His skin was yellowed, and his movements appeared painful. Travers had heard about the mayor's drinking problems and his mean temper. His early life as a coal miner had probably been arduous. Now, in his late fifties, he had lived a hard life. He was undoubtedly slowing down, but not fast enough for the Outfit.

Cermak was well-guarded. Travers had seen them when he got off the train in Miami. The platform had been cleared as Cermak walked confidently, surrounded by a crew of five bodyguards. He might have been wearing the protective vest, but the mayor was a big man with or without the vest padding. If someone wanted to shoot him, they would have to shoot between the bodyguards or toss a grenade. He was not an easy target.

Due to their spying activities at the dog track, Zak and Ethan had taken turns following Zangara around the city. The man never noticed them; their tracking was successful, but whether it was productive or not remained unknown. Playing the dogs was not a crime, nor was his relationship with Ethan's new friend, Angela, regardless of Ethan's sensitivities. Two nights ago, Ethan had stopped by the Kennel Club and picked up Angela after work. Again, he asked some questions about her cousin, Giuseppe Zangara. This time she was very defensive, according to Ethan. She was so upset that he decided to drop the subject. But now, this strange man had taken on another dimension. According to Zak, he bought a gun at a pawn shop this afternoon and then returned to his hotel room. When Travers heard about the gun, he told Zak and Ethan to stop surveillance. He knew that Ethan had another date with Angela tonight, and he warned Ethan to be very careful.

As Travers combed his hair, someone knocked loudly on his door. He wrapped the towel around his waist like a sarong and answered the door. He was expecting a bellboy with an envelope containing tickets for tonight's show; instead, he found a rather imposing young man. No older than Ethan or Zak, he was tall and built like a boxer, and he wore a baby face that looked as if he had spent some time in the ring. His sharkskin suit, white shirt, tie, and diamond stick pin were complemented by the obligatory fedora. He looked like a Hollywood mobster, like a kid playing the part. He boldly stepped into the room without speaking, forcing Travers to step backward, awkwardly hanging onto his bath towel. A large, menacing goon followed.

"Gentlemen," said Travers. "Welcome to my humble abode. Please come right in. Make yourselves at home. I'm afraid you caught me slightly underdressed for the occasion."

"Funny man," said the first man, looking at the second. "Dave Yaras. You heard of me?"

Travers nodded. "I'm good with names. Mr. Nitti mentioned you would be looking after me. Is that the reason for the personal audience?"

"Right. That's the reason. I understand you're untouchable."

"I hope so..." said Travers with a smile.

Yaras didn't return the smile. "Stop talkin' and just listen. I really don't give a damn who you are. This visit is really about me, my friend. I got a job to do, and I gotta do it well or else I'll be fired. Now, the boss can tell me to do it while ridin' on an elephant. And I'll tell him that's no problem. But, in real life, that's just chatter. I'm not goin' to ride a goddamn elephant, Travers. You made a deal. You said you'd keep your nose out of our business. But you and your friends' noses have been all over this town."

"May I sit down? It's getting a little breezy in here."

"Sit," said the mobster as he bounced on his toes, "Suit yourself. Just listen to me."

Travers sat on the edge of the bed, looking up at Yaras. The goon stood against the door facing him. His jacket was open just enough to expose a .38 in a holster.

"I'm listening," said Travers. He knew this was all a show. If they wanted to rough him up, they would have done it by now. He would play his part and wasn't about to poke at these two snakes.

"Your idiot friends have been playing pretend games.

Newspaper reporters. Poker players. Detectives. You think they wouldn't be noticed? You think I didn't put two and two together? The trail leads right back to this hotel and to you."

Travers waited. He wanted to be sure this wasn't a rhetorical question. It wasn't. Yaras wanted an answer. "OK, Dave. You said you had a job to do. You work for the man. Well, I have a job to do also. I work for my man. I needed to make sure things would go as planned. I asked my friends to do some checking. Obviously, that was a mistake. You're on top of things. Fine. But you see, your boss didn't provide me with your phone number and address. So this was the only way I could make sure that we talked."

"What?"

Travers got up. "Bear with me for a second. I just want to put on a pair of pants and a shirt. OK?"

"No B.S., Travers. Primo Carnera here will be keeping an eye on you."

Travers found his clothes and donned them. Then he sat down on one of the two chairs in the room. The distant sound of buoy bells, carried in on a warm ocean breeze from the bay, drifted in the open window. Travers took a deep breath before speaking. "Much better. If I'm going to meet my maker, I want to look my best."

Yaras paced back and forth as if he didn't know exactly what to do or say. Finally, he turned and faced Travers. "OK. I'll bite. What's your game?"

"Look. I get it. As far as I'm concerned, you're the law in this town. I know you have a job to do. Not a very nice job, but that's not for me to say. I just have one point to make."

"Go ahead. Make it."

"You've been a boxer, right?"

"You've done your homework. So?"

"My boy has to come out of this standing up. He's got to look like a winner. No bruises. No bumps. No cuts. You have the bells and whistles to make that happen. I have no idea what your plans are. But I do not want you to even wrinkle Mr. Roosevelt's suit. I don't have to remind you that your previous boss has made a federal prison his home. The deck is stacked against you. You can't fight the national police force and the United States Army. So, even if you succeed in eliminating your foe, you will fail at this job...if you fail to protect my boss. Does that make sense?

"You threatenin' me?"

"No. Just reminding you of the obvious. In the heat of action, you might go against your best interests and those of your boss. I'm not a threat to you. I promised not to interfere. I will not interfere. Frank Nitti promised me that you would respect my position. Do what you will, but Mr. Roosevelt must not be harmed."

Dave Yaras looked at Travers dead on. His blood was rising and filling his eyes with anger. He looked like a boxer who had just been cut and tasted his own blood. He wiped his mouth with the back of his hand as he took one step forward. Travers stayed easy in his chair. Yaras stopped and wagged his finger at him. Almost shouting, he blew up. "You're screwin' with me. You want a war?"

Travers sat immobile. He stared down the rabid dog. Yaras stood motionless. Seconds passed. Then the blood slowly moved out of the mobster's face, and his neck shrunk back to normal. Travers made no show of his own emotion. He grabbed a pack of cigarettes and, carefully and with a steady hand, he bounced one up. With practiced movements, he brought the pack up to his mouth, his lips gently grabbed the end of a cigarette, and he returned the pack to his shirt pocket. He lit the cigarette and took a stiff drag. The nicotine hit reinforced him, and he exhaled nonchalantly toward the ceiling. He hoped his routine would not have the appearance of indifference or disrespect. He knew Dave Yaras was a brutal man. He was a certified killer; as young as he was, he was one of the Outfit's most reliable hitmen. Travers only wanted him to see the larger view. If he could imprint this message onto this beast of a man, he would consider the evening a success.

"All right, Jack Travers. You made your point. And I made mine. But get your little buddies out of my face. Or I may forget my better self. Deal?"

"I will instruct them to stop."

"Do they know the real story?"

Travers answered quickly. "They don't have the slightest idea."

"Keep it that way."

"Right. Except one thing."

Yaras made a face. "What's that?"

"My friend, the big guy. I think he's fallen for that Angela girl. She works at the Kennel Club as a hat-check girl."

"So?"

"I may not be able to keep him away from her. You know...young people in love."

"I know everyone at the Kennel Club. I'll take care of her. But that's my business. This will all be over soon. Behave yourself, Travers."

"One more question..."

"Yeah?"

"The little guy we've been tailing. Zangara. Is he one of your people?"

"You don't really want to know the details, do you?"

Jack thought for a moment. "No, I don't. I'll just assume you have everything under control, including the gun that guy bought today."

Yaras took two quick steps forward and stood over Jack. "You're really pushing me. Just keep your nose out of this. Go dancin' tonight. It's Valentine's Day. Treat your girlfriend right. Keep her and her friends out of this, and nobody will get hurt except those who deserve it."

Travers's stomach tightened when he realized that Yaras might be threatening Emma.

The mobster reached into his jacket pocket and pulled out an envelope. "I forgot to give this to you. I told the bellboy you and I were friends. Don't worry. He got a nice tip."

Travers took the envelope containing the tickets.

The goon opened the door, and Yaras turned and marched through. Primo Carnera gave Travers a primitive, ugly, and unforgettable look as he followed his boss out the door. Travers stared blankly and took another deep drag from his Lucky.

Fifteen minutes later, the entire group of time travelers and Jack Travers held a meeting in his room. The smell of the mobsters' cheap cologne still lingered in the air. Travers explained that their investigative mission was over. It was too dangerous for them to do anything but wait it out. He also told Ethan that he should stay away from Angela until Franklin Roosevelt was on a train heading north. Even then, it might be risky, explained Travers, because no one could predict the actions of a man like Dave Yaras.

Ethan was upset. "Let me get this straight. You don't want to do anything else. You want us to just sit around and wait and see what happens? And you two," he looked at his sister and Travers, "are going out for an evening on the town? This is crazy. Anyway, if I want to see Angela again, I will."

"Look, Ethan. Yaras and his people are watching us. All of us. If they see Emma and me out having fun, they'll relax. I really don't want to rile them. I have made my point, and I'm certain they understand. I am confident now that however they act, they will act in consideration of Mr. Roosevelt's safety. We won't have to do anything else. As a matter of fact, we could endanger Mr. Roosevelt if we interfere at this point. You've done your job, and I thank you. The circle is complete. Everyone is clear."

"Well, we're interested in FDR's safety also. Maybe more than you."

"I doubt that, Ethan." Travers looked to Emma for help.

Emma put one hand on Travers's shoulder. "I think

we have to trust Jack. He's the expert here," she said.

Zak stood up and signed. *"What about Zangara? We've been following him around for three days. Doesn't anyone think it's suspicious that he just bought a gun and ten bullets?"*

Emma looked at Currant, who had been silent up to this point. She translated. "He's concerned about Zangara."

Currant straightened. "I am too. I think we should keep an eye on him. We don't really know what's motivating him. Jack, how can you just assume that your mobster buddies are the only dangerous people in town? What if Zangara has something planned on his own? What if he had it in his mind to shoot FDR?"

"You mean the mobsters are planning to get rid of Cermak, and somebody is also planning to shoot FDR?" asked Jack.

"It's possible."

"I suppose anything is possible. But it's pretty clear that Zangara is working for the Outfit. What possible motive could he have for attacking Roosevelt?"

"Lone nut," said Currant.

"What?"

"The guy could just be a nut. You don't know. That guy who shot President McKinley was a nut. And what about that fellow who killed President Garfield?"

"As far as I know, the guy who shot Garfield had a personal grudge," replied Jack. "And the guy who shot McKinley was a dedicated anarchist. You think Zangara ever met Roosevelt? You think he's an anarchist? I think he's a guy who plays the dogs and horses and loses. I think he's a low-level nobody who may be involved. According to Ethan's friend Angela, he's in debt. He's a drifter. He's a loser. Yes, I think he's involved...with the Outfit."

"Maybe so. But we should watch him," said Currant. "The whole thing could boil over into a terrible accident. He could shoot at Cermak and hit Roosevelt by mistake. How can we be sure that wouldn't happen?" Ethan and

Zak nodded their agreement.

Jack Travers was frustrated. "The people we're dealing with are experts. And they know their limitations. Please. I know it was my idea to get you involved. Maybe that was a mistake. In the end, no one was fooled. And I got you involved in a dangerous situation. For that, I'm sorry. But, please. Drop it now. OK?"

Currant looked at Zak and Ethan. "All right, Jack. We understand. Have a nice time tonight."

Jack nodded. He reached out to Emma. "Let's go have some fun, Emma. The night is young."

Chapter XVIII

The Contract

On the evening of February 14th, Dave Yaras was a busy man. And his to-do list was growing. Still upset after visiting Travers, he struggled to keep his anger intact. Walking through the hotel lobby, he heard his name paged repeatedly. It unnerved him. He located the squawking bellboy, who handed him an envelope. Instinctively, he wanted to question the kid, but instead, he just tossed him a quarter and read the note: *Mr. Yaras, please call me immediately. My clients have a significant business opportunity for your evaluation. Thomas Coleman, Attorney at Law.*

He told his goon to wait while he made a phone call to his personal attorney, an old-time shyster who knew Miami and how to keep a secret. Yaras was wary. He asked his mouthpiece if he recognized the law firm. He did. According to him, they only handled corporate law.

"Big-time clients. They own or run half of the Caribbean. Bananas, sugar, cigars, stuff like that. If you're asking me if these guys are legit...the answer is yes."

Yaras made a snap decision, hung up, and called the other number. The conversation was short. Yaras was intrigued and told him he could meet up in ten minutes.

The attorney's office was near the new federal building, just west of Travers' hotel. The two mobsters rode the steel-cage elevator to the third floor of the building and exited into the semi-darkness of the open corridor. The folding gate shut, its sound echoing loudly. Besides the sleepy guard at the front door, the place appeared empty. Across the atrium, there was one lighted office. The clear glass door offered a view inside. Coleman's name was one of many gold-leafed on the glass. They entered, Yaras pointed to a chair, and his goon sat. Then a man in a white shirt and a tie walked out of one of the offices.

"Mr. Yaras?"

Yaras nodded.

"Come into my office, please."

In his early thirties, the thin man with slicked-down black hair, a pencil mustache, hollow cheeks, and delicate features looked harmless. Yaras followed him.

"Do you mind if I close the door?"

Yaras checked out the office. "Sure. My friend outside will keep an eye on things."

"Fine. Have a seat, Mr. Yaras."

Yaras sat as the attorney eased into his wood-and-leather swivel chair and turned to face him.

"I do appreciate that you have come here on such short notice. But some things have an immediacy about them."

"What things?" He glanced side to side and tapped his knotty fingers on the desktop.

Coleman smiled. "I see you are a man who gets to the point, Mr. Yaras."

"Yeah. What's on your mind? I've got a lot on mine."

"So I have heard."

"What have you heard?" Yaras edged forward in the chair. "Wait a second. I don't want no ears on this." He walked to the door. Swinging it open, he told the goon to stand outside the entry door. The man did as told. Yaras backtracked and sat. "OK. I'm listening, Coleman."

"All good things, all good things." He leaned forward and spoke softly. "I represent a consortium that would like to make a one-time purchase of your services. They have received word that you have a mission this week. An assignment to eliminate impediments to successfully operating your principal's business interests in Chicago."

Yaras took a moment to digest the words. "Say again."

Very quietly, Coleman mouthed the words. "Mr.

Cermak."

"Humph," Yaras shook his head. "Three men can keep a secret if two of them are dead," he mumbled. The fact that this attorney knew that Cermak was on borrowed time was not a great surprise. Many people on the inside could make that assumption, but this guy knew it was happening this week and that Yaras was in charge. Few people knew that.

The attorney opened the gold-plated cigarette box on his desk.

"Cigarette?"

Yaras accepted, and the attorney lit both cigarettes. Yaras picked a piece of tobacco from his lower lip and flicked it off his finger onto the floor. "You know... assumin' I know what you're talkin' about, why would I talk to you? As you say, this is something my 'principal' would decide. Not me."

"Well, Mr. Yaras. These services my clients seek would probably not be approved by your employer."

"Why the hell would I discuss anything with you? I'm not about to throw a rabbit punch at my boss."

Coleman nodded. "Everything I say to you is in the strictest confidence, and I hope you will reciprocate. It would not be in anyone's best interest to reveal our conversation. However, no matter what happens tonight, you will have gained some important friends. The benefit of your silence regarding this conversation will become obvious. You are loyal; that makes sense. Your people have their secrets, and mine have theirs. But in this case, you may want to hear me out. Just give me a few minutes to explain my side. All right?

Yaras nodded.

"First, I cannot tell you who I represent. But I can say that my clients have considerable power and wealth. And they are not pleased with the current political situation. Mr. Cermak is of no interest to them except as a means to an end. They do not favor Mr. Roosevelt. It is their desire that he not be allowed to assume a position of national power."

Yaras sucked on his cigarette and blew out a heavy blast of smoke. He shifted in his chair and gave the attorney a wary look.

Coleman appeared to sense his uneasiness. "Hear me out. Our offer will in no way compromise your mission. And you will receive a payment of fifty thousand dollars."

Dave Yaras considered the attorney's offer. His eyes shifted then returned to the eyes of the other man. "So I want to get this straight. You want me to eliminate your problem. I can still take care of my boss's problem, and I'll get fifty grand for my trouble."

The attorney offered a faint smile. "That's right. We would expect that the entire operation would be folded into one event. Everything would appear to happen simultaneously. Is that possible?"

Yaras thought. He scratched his head. "It's possible. But I don't like this. My people have made a point of making sure Roosevelt remains untouched."

"Ah. Yes. That's why we are offering a great amount of money...just to you."

"Look. I don't care about either of these guys. But I obey orders. That money will only buy me a fancier funeral. Why knock out Roosevelt? He hasn't even had time to make a mess of anything."

Coleman relaxed. "That's a good question. I can tell you that he was not even supposed to be a candidate. But, he is quite the politician. He surprised everyone. Now he's won the election, and he's not a go-along kind of guy, Dave. He's going to socialize America, and he will destroy the economy. What we need now is a strong leader. The country's problems are too great. We need someone like a Mussolini or a Hitler."

Yaras chuckled. "You kiddin'? Those guys are certifiable."

Coleman nodded. "I agree, but we'll find a distinctly American version. Someone the people will trust and someone who will work with the great corporations to ensure that the 'business of America will be business.'

My clients can't take a chance on the future of this country. This man Roosevelt is a traitor to his class. And just so you know, the first thing he will do when he is in office will be to eliminate the Prohibition laws. So I don't think anyone will miss him. Certainly not your employers."

Yaras thought. "Makes sense." He stubbed out his cigarette. "If this could be made to happen, when do I get paid?"

Coleman smiled, slid open a desk drawer, and pulled out an envelope. He placed it on the desk in front of Yaras. "Take a look. As I said, it's a one-time payment."

Yaras looked in the envelope. It was unsealed, and inside was a stack of thousand-dollar bills. "All large," mumbled Yaras.

"I'm sure you can find someone to make change." He smiled.

"So what keeps me from taking this and walking out the door, leaving you with egg on your face?"

Coleman laughed. "Nothing. Absolutely nothing. But my clients are resourceful, if you know what I mean, just like your people. A handshake is a deal. I would suggest you be very careful with this payment. You wouldn't want to bring attention to yourself. If, for some reason, you make an honest effort but fail in your task, you keep the retainer. And you keep your silence."

"Who's to judge whether I made the effort?

The attorney pursed his lips. "You're a man of integrity. I don't think that would be a problem. And, of course, you must establish a convincing scenario. It wouldn't be in anyone's best interest if it looked like you or your men were involved in any way. If you fail to do that, I don't think you will have the opportunity to be concerned about our opinion."

Yaras thumbed through the bills but didn't remove them from the envelope. He held his thoughts for a long count.

"Take your time, but this is a one-time offer. It won't be on the table tomorrow."

Yaras nodded. His mind was a blur. If Nitti found out he took the money, he would be a dead man. But fifty thousand was ten times the going rate, an incredible amount for one night's work. He only had to make an attempt as far as he could tell. One shot—in the right direction. Hit or miss, he would be in the clear. He thought about having somebody else do the deed, but that would only make it tougher to keep a lid on things. Either he did it himself, or it wouldn't happen. His best bet would be to succeed.

There wouldn't be much of an investigation. Especially if the cops found out that one of FDR's own people, Jack Travers, was aware of the hit on Cermak. This one would get buried by the Roosevelt people. It was too hot to handle. Yaras would use the same caliber of weapon that Zangara would fire, but his gun would have a suppressor. With all the crowd noise and fear in the air, no one would notice him or the muffled sound of his shot. The investigators would have their patsy. Giuseppe Zangara would take the fall. One stinkin' shot. He smiled at the attorney.

"All right, Coleman. I'm in. I think I can find a way to make everything happen at once. I got a guy I'm putting on the spot to take the heat. And then he'll be out of the picture. He's set up to look like the only guy involved. Can't be helped if he makes a mistake and takes out two guys instead of one."

Coleman smiled. His little black mustache curled upward. He nodded his head. "Things like that happen."

Yaras grabbed the envelope from the desktop. He used his tongue to seal it, then slipped it into his inside jacket pocket. They both stood.

"One thing, Coleman."

"Yes."

"No one ever hears anything about this. Right?"

"My clients have no reason to say anything to anyone. And I am bound by the attorney-client privilege."

"I know you'll keep your mouth shut."

Coleman nodded and swallowed hard. He extended

his hand. "Mr. Yaras..."

"Huh."

"We need to shake on the deal." They shook hands. "I will tell my clients that their offer has been made. That you have accepted it. That they have satisfied their obligation. And you will satisfy your end of the deal tomorrow evening. You'll do a good job, Mr. Yaras. I'm sure you will."

Dave Yaras left the attorney's office and traveled to a safe house run by a friend. The building was a garage for truck repair, with a second floor built as a small apartment. Two men who had traveled from Chicago were waiting for him. These were Nitti's boys, dependable and experienced: Frankie Rio and Three Fingers Jack White. He had met them before. Yaras left his bodyguard sitting at the wheel of his car, parked behind the building. He grabbed a package from the trunk and tucked it under his arm. As he walked up the exterior stairs to the second-floor landing, he worked out what he would say to the two hoods. He wanted to make sure they were totally focused on their jobs. If so, with the adrenaline flowing, Zangara shooting, and the crowd going crazy with fear and excitement, they wouldn't notice him firing his silenced gun at Roosevelt.

Yaras knocked on the door: one knock, a pause, then four more. Rio, always dapper, was wearing a silk shirt and white linen pants as he opened the door and let him in. Jack White, balding and appearing much older than his thirty-three years, immediately handed him a juice glass partially filled with whiskey. Yaras set the package on the kitchen counter.

"Three fingers of rye, Jack?" quipped Yaras. Jack White, who sported only three fingers on his left hand, smiled briefly at the attempted humor. "It's a joke, Jack. Let's drink up." The three men shared a bottle of booze and small-talked. Yaras was more than a decade younger than the two hoods sent down from Chicago, and he was wary of them. They were an unknown and dangerous quantity. Yaras' assignment was to set the table and stay out of the way. He reached for the package and flipped the top off the rectangular box, exposing its contents. "There you go, boys. You're now officially Cicero cops, badges and all."

"We're supposed to wear these?" asked White.

"They arrived yesterday. Somebody in Chicago thinks these costumes are a good idea."

Rio lifted one of the police uniforms and held it up. It proved to only be suitable for a taller man. "This might work for you, Jack, but I'd look like a clown in it." He checked the second one. "Same size. This monkey suit ain't gonna work."

White held up a uniform. "I can wear this. I guess. So. What's the plan?" He looked at Yaras, who was instantly reassessing the mechanics of the hit.

"The pigeon, Joe Zangara, will do the deed."

"Is he reliable?" asked Rio.

Yaras smiled. "Let's put it this way. I gave him no choice. He knows he's a walkin' dead man. He'll do it. He's got no options. If he does this, he might have some chance to live. Even if he doesn't live, there are other people that he's soft on. I gave him a line of B.S. I told him we won't bother them, and if he delivers, we'd forget the money he owes us and toss in a grand for him. Tickets to Cuba for him and his girlfriend. He's in the bag."

"Better have an escort for him. He might get cold feet," said Three Fingers.

"I got someone who will make sure he gets to Bayfront Park. They'll get there early so Zangara can find a good place to shoot from. One of you will be there to take care of him after he shoots. And one of you will be near Cermak to make sure he's hit. One way or the other. Jack, since you fit the uniform, maybe you should take a position somewhere near the stage. Everyone who's anyone will be sittin' up there, including Cermak."

"What's this Joe guy packin'?"

"He's got a .32. Ten rounds."

"How the hell is he going to kill anyone with that peashooter?"

"It's a five-shot. I told him he's gotta empty it. Maybe he'll hit Cermak. Maybe he won't. But you will, Jack. Just stay out of his line of fire. He was in the Italian army. So he knows somethin' about guns. But I wouldn't take any chances," said Yaras.

"I don't shoot nobody with that piece of crap," said White. He pulled a .38 revolver from his holster. "This will do the job. If I get close enough. But it's a .38."

Yaras shook his head. "Who cares? If he's dead, he's dead."

Rio paced the room listening to the conversation, then stopped in place. "How do I finger Zangara? The place is gonna be jammed."

Yaras pulled his wallet from his jacket vest pocket and removed a small photo. "Here's what he looks like."

Frankie Rio laughed. "I'm supposed to find this guy somewhere in the middle of thousands of people? He's what? Five feet tall? You want me to stalk him all night so I don't lose him?"

Yaras shook his head. "Not a good idea. We don't want to spook him. I got a broad who will be right by his side. She'll stick to him like glue. She'll be wearin' a yellow dress and a big floppy yellow hat with a pink ribbon on it. A looker, and tall, too. You'll spot her from a mile, and she's not goin' to leave him."

The men discussed the details of the operation, including their escape from the area after the shooting. By the time they finished talking, the bottle was empty. Yaras said he might be watching tomorrow night. But that was all. "It's your thing, guys." He checked his watch. It was just after ten. He had to go. "We'll meet here again tomorrow at five o'clock sharp." Yaras grabbed the extra police uniform and left.

He hopped in his car and told the driver to make time, and they sped across the bay bridge leading to Miami Beach. A big moon floated low over the ocean, reflecting on the rolling waves. He tossed a cigarette butt out the window. It bounced off the concrete, sparking before it fell into the water. Yaras checked his watch— *10:18*. It was coming together, he thought. By this time tomorrow night, it would be all over. Two men would be dead, and the country would be in shock. Hopefully, Frank Nitti would be happy, and Dave Yaras would be a rich man. They drove east through the side streets of Miami Beach. He had told Angela to wait for him at the entrance to the dog track. She left work early and was waiting at the curb when they arrived. She looked nervous and got in at his command, and they drove on. As they cruised the streets of Miami Beach, he talked, and she listened.

Twenty minutes later, the car pulled up in front of Angela's apartment building. She popped out, slammed the car door, and ran into the building.

-Chapter XIX-

An Insurance Policy

A few minutes later, Ethan went to the Kennel Club to meet Angela after work. He waited in front, but she didn't show. He asked around. The doorman at the racetrack entrance knew Angela. He saw her stay outside the gate waiting, then she got into the backseat of a car. He claimed he didn't know who was driving.

Ethan found a phone booth and telephoned Angela's apartment building. The phone rang and rang, but no one answered. He tried again. This time a man answered who wasn't interested in helping. Ethan told him it was imperative. He begged him to find Angela. Reluctantly, he agreed to knock on her apartment door. In the background, the radio had Rudy Vallee singing "Brother, Can You Spare a Dime?" Ethan was nervous. He waited. Finally, the song at its end, he heard her voice.

"I'm so happy to get you. I waited for you. You were gone. I was told you got a ride from some men. Are you all right?"

She seemed out of breath. "Ethan, I'm sorry. I can't talk. I can't see you. You must leave me alone."

"What? Angela, what are you saying? Have you been crying?"

She didn't answer, but Ethan could hear her muffled cries. "Maybe..." She sniffled. "Ethan, don't worry about me. I'll be fine. It's just that I can't see you for a couple of days. Something important has come up. You understand. Don't you? It's too late tonight."

"I know it's late, Angela. But I want to see you. Can't we just meet for a few minutes?"

"No."

"Then when? How about tomorrow morning? We could have breakfast. First thing. We can meet at that little coffee shop up your street. The place with the wooden Indian out front. I'll be there at nine. If you're not there, I'll just walk to your building. Either way, we'll get together. We can talk. OK?"

"Ethan, I need you." She stopped sobbing. "I do want to see you. I'll meet you tomorrow morning. If I'm not on time, just wait for me."

"OK. And Angela..."

"Yes."

"I love you." The words eased out of Ethan's mouth without thought. Then they bounced around in his head but had no place to land. He felt very young and foolish.

"Tomorrow," she said as if she hadn't heard those words. She hung up.

Slowly, Ethan replaced the receiver, opened the telephone booth door, and stepped out. In the distance, breakers crashed. For a moment, he stood motionless, frozen in thought. He looked up at the moon rising over the Atlantic. Something was very wrong with Angela. But he would have to wait. There was nothing he could do now.

When he got back to his hotel, Currant was gone. Ethan went to a nearby speakeasy for a nightcap. But Zak was there and eager to know if he had learned more about Zangara. Ethan didn't tell him about Angela and the car. He said he could not meet with Angela but would meet her tomorrow morning. With that, he returned to his room. Emma was not there. He knew she wouldn't return until morning. He got ready for bed, but sleep didn't come easy. Only one thing was on his mind, and it wasn't. Zangara, Roosevelt, or Yaras, it was Angela. He tossed about, listening to the night sounds outside his open window. In time, sleep captured him.

The next day he waited for her at the coffee shop. He stood next to the Indian figure and looked inside. The place was packed with people, but she was not there. He looked at the wooden Indian, then his watch. He wasn't about to wait.

In five minutes, he was at the door of her apartment. He knocked. He heard some rustling inside, then she opened the door. She wore a nightgown, her hair was unkempt, her eyes red, and her cheeks streaked with tears. She threw herself at him, and they embraced. She cried. As he entered, he gently kicked the door shut.

"My papa. They have him," she sobbed.

He pulled away. "Sit down." He moved her to the sofa. He found an open bottle of grappa in a kitchen cupboard, filled the bottom of a glass with the brown liquid, and handed it to her. "Drink this."

She took the glass and sipped it while he walked to the bedroom. The bed was a mess. Things had been knocked off the dresser and lay on the floor; shutters and curtains on the windows remained closed. He returned to her side and put his arm around her. "What happened?"

She drank slowly, coughed, and got control of her breathing. "He came in the middle of the night and took papa."

"Who came?"

"Dave Yaras' guy. That big, ugly man. I opened the door. He pushed his way in. He pulled papa out of bed. Told him to get dressed. I grabbed at him and hit him with a hairbrush. But he just shook me off onto the floor. He said my father was an 'insurance policy. That I should do my job. But if I didn't....'" She swallowed hard and fought back her tears. "He ran his finger across his throat."

"Yaras is a mobster, right?"

She looked up at him. "You know him?"

"I know who he is. What is he to you? Tell me the whole story."

She thought for a moment. "If I tell you...you must promise not to tell anyone. They will kill my father. You must promise."

"Angela, just tell me. You know I want to help you."

"OK. This is all about Giuseppe Zangara."

"Your cousin."

She leaned into the back of the sofa. She looked down. "He's not my cousin. He was born in the same region as my father, but we're not related. He's a guy I met at the dog track. I should say I was told to meet him."

"By Yaras?"

"Yes."

"How do you know Yaras?"

"Everyone at the club knows him. He's probably an owner. He acts like it. I don't know for sure. But he bosses people around. Including me."

"I get it."

"I had to make like I'm enjoying meeting Zangara. I don't know why, but Yaras wanted it. I'm not going to argue with him. So I did. Zangara seemed to like me. We went out for drinks. He isn't a bad guy. But he's a *nessuno*...a nobody. He asked me to call him Joe. It seemed like he was trying hard to be liked. As far as I know, he doesn't have any friends. He kept returning to the track and spent a lot of money. At first, I thought he was just a pigeon. You know, somebody they want to gamble away their money. But after a time, I figured out he works for Yaras."

"So you dated this Zangara guy?"

She grabbed his forearm lightly. "It's not like that. We just spent time with each other. It seemed harmless. You know...jobs don't grow on trees these days. I'm only a hat-check girl, but it's a job."

Ethan nodded. "OK. What's next?"

"Last night, Yaras picked me up and told me I had to do something else."

"What?"

"I have to meet Joe at Bayfront Park tonight at 8 o'clock. I'm supposed to be wearing my yellow dress and a silly sunbonnet. A sunbonnet at night...." She made a face. "I've got to stay with him all night. There's supposed to be a crowd of people to hear someone speak. And I'm supposed to help him get a good seat and stay with him to the end. He said if I didn't, he would make my life miserable. And my father's, too."

Ethan got up and paced the room. She was in the middle of it now. He had to do something. "You know what's happening there tonight?"

"No."

"Franklin Roosevelt is making a speech."

She looked at him with disbelief. "I didn't know." She looked frightened now, as if the pieces were falling together in her head.

"Angela, you're in the middle of something big. That's why they took your father. Zangara works for Yaras. He's going to shoot somebody tonight. They want him to kill the mayor of Chicago. That's why he's going there. That's why they want you there. You knew that, right?"

She broke down and cried. Ethan attempted to console her, but then she lost it. After the crying stopped, she dried her tears with his handkerchief. "I knew they wanted me to lie to him. They said he wanted to take me to Cuba. I'm supposed to say I'll go with him. But I would never do that. Especially now. This is *pazzo*. Crazy."

"What do you mean by 'especially now'?"

"I mean, since I met you." She paused. "What am I saying? I would never go anywhere with that man."

"Did Yaras suggest you and I get together?"

She looked into his eyes. "I wouldn't lie to you. Somehow he knew about you and your sister. For some reason, he was pushing it. But I didn't need him to make me like you. I liked you from the start."

"Well, seems like Dave Yaras is everyone's fairy godmother."

"What?"

"Forget it." His mind refocused on his original mission. "Listen, Angela. We're going to get through this. For the moment, just do what he asks. I'll be nearby every minute tonight. You won't be alone. I really don't want you helping Joe Zangara in any way. It's bad enough that you're involved to this extent. If something bad happens, you could be implicated."

"What about my papa?"

"Right. I would say he's safe. For now. But we need to get him away from Yaras. Do you have any idea where they've taken him?"

"I don't know. How would I know?"

"Do you know where Yaras lives? Or where his office is?"

"No. I only saw him at the club."

"What about Zangara?"

"What?"

"Do you know where he lives?"

She paused before answering. "He took me to his apartment once. He lives in an attic room. Above a house. I was just there for a couple of minutes."

"Do you remember where it is?"

"Sure. I remember. 5th Street. Five or six blocks off of Biscayne Boulevard. Do you think that's where they have my father?"

"I don't know."

"That man who took my papa. He told him not to worry. He said my father would have company. Maybe he was talking about Zangara. I'm wondering whether Zangara wants to use my father as bait. He knows I wouldn't go anywhere without him. Maybe he will try to talk him into going to Cuba."

"I want you to clean up and get dressed. We're going for a taxi ride. I want to know exactly where Zangara's place is located. And don't worry about your father. We'll get him back."

She reached out and hugged Ethan. He felt her close to him, and, like a little wounded animal, she burrowed her head into his shoulder. His feelings for her hadn't changed. She was caught in a trap. It was his job to release its jaws.

With renewed energy, Angela prepared for the day. They left the apartment and walked west, catching a taxi at the next intersection. Ten minutes later, they rode along 5th Street in Miami, a mix of older houses, offices, and stores waiting to be demolished in the next building boom and recast as downtown frontage. They neared the end of the block.

"Slow down," she ordered the driver. "That's it," she said. She pointed to a stained white stucco two-story residence heavily laden with vegetation. "See those stairs next to the driveway? They lead to the attic apartment."

"We might get lucky, Angela. I'm going to stick around. I'll watch this place."

Ethan looked hard to see any signs of Yaras or his goon. But the driveway was empty, and the upstairs windows were closed. He told the cab driver to drop him off at the end of the block. And he asked Angela not to worry. It was best if they weren't seen together. He and his friends would try to find her father. Even if they failed to find him, Yaras would not need her father after tonight. Tonight she should do just as Yaras asked. It would all be over by ten o'clock. He said he would watch over her to ensure no harm came to her. He promised this with a kiss.

The taxi pulled away. Ethan knew it was a long shot that Angela's father was being held in Zangara's apartment. But unless Travers had any ideas, it was anyone's guess where Angela's dad might have been taken. He found a spot where he could watch the house unobserved and waited.

Frustration set in. After watching the house for over an hour, Ethan was not a patient man. There was no movement inside or out. He wanted to leave. As much as he was concerned about Angela and her father, there was little he could do. Yaras could have taken the old man out of town for all he knew. But he decided to give it ten more minutes. Then as he spotted a big black car approaching, he ducked behind a tree.

The car pulled into the driveway, and Dave Yaras got out. He had a paper bag in his hand. He glanced around, and then, apparently satisfied that he wasn't being watched, he bounced up the wooden steps, opened the door, and entered the apartment. A few minutes later, he returned, got in his car, and left the way he came. Now confident this was where Angela's father was being held, Ethan returned to his hotel to meet with the others.

Chapter XX

Spider Web

When Ethan arrived at the hotel, Emma and Jack Travers sat in the lobby. Emma looked relieved to see him. Travers looked at his watch. "It's almost noon. We all need to talk. Where were you this morning, Ethan?"

"I went to see Angela. Listen, I have some news." He was excited.

"All right. Hang on. I'll put a call into A.C.'s room, and we'll all get together." Travers went to the hotel desk and grabbed a house phone. He returned. "They're coming."

A.C. Currant, Zak, Ethan, Emma, and Jack Travers assembled in the lobby, and then as a group, they left the hotel and headed for Bayfront Park. A nearby roadway intersecting Biscayne Boulevard led directly east to the water. Halfway between was a gazebo. The young couple embracing in the shade of the building was startled by their approach. When the five strangers ambled up the steps, they departed for more private surroundings.

It was a pleasant spot. Sitting on a bench facing the water, Ethan surveyed the tree-lined road, which terminated at the water's edge. Sailboats, anchored in the bay, bobbed in the breeze, and freighters slowly plied the Atlantic in the distance. To his right, directly on axis with the gazebo, and a few hundred feet distant, stood the boxy yellow stucco stage building that would be the site of FDR's speech tonight. The hot afternoon sun bounced off the Byzantine-style building's three onion domes, making them stand out like dollops of frosting atop a cupcake. The outdoor stage area was in front of the stage building.

Aside from the strange design of the building, it was

an ideal spot for an outdoor gathering. The expansive semicircular arrangement of seats in front of the stage could seat thousands of people. Ethan thought about tonight's rally. The perfect Miami weather would bring out a crowd. Announcements and location maps had appeared in today's newspapers, and people wanted to see the next President of the United States. It was a rare opportunity to witness history. But each of the five visitors sitting inside the gazebo this early afternoon knew it could end in tragedy.

Ethan sat in the middle, with Emma and Jack to his left and Dr. Currant and Zak to his right. "What's up, Ethan? Emma tells me you met with Angela this morning. Did she give you any clue about Zangara?" asked Currant.

"Yes, we…"

Travers interrupted. "Before we get into Ethan's story, let's all remember that we're here to witness history, not to make history. I hope that is clear. An unfortunate event is coming. But it's not one of our doing. It's a tribal squabble between mob rivals. I believe my deal will remain intact. Tonight, I would like you to stay well away from the proceedings. I don't want anyone to get hurt."

Ethan jumped up. "You haven't heard my story, Jack. You may change your mind after hearing it. Let me talk, OK?"

"Go ahead. I didn't mean to run roughshod over you."

"Thanks. I met with Angela this morning. She's involved in this whole thing. Not by her choice. She was threatened into participating. Apparently, Dave Yaras instigated a make-believe relationship between her and this fellow Zangara. The whole idea was to gain his confidence. To make promises to him. Money, Angela, escape to Cuba. Live happily ever after. You get the picture. The important thing is that Zangara is Yaras's man. He'll be here tonight. He will attempt to kill Mayor Cermak."

"Ethan, what about Angela? Why don't we just get

her and keep her out of trouble?" asked Emma.

"Because...Yaras has kidnapped her father. And he's threatened to kill him if Angela doesn't cooperate with all his schemes. Also, I think I was set up. I think Yaras arranged to have Angela and I meet. He wants to tie me to you and Jack and us to the crime. She will be involved in the action. I am involved with her. And you are involved with me. The Outfit set us up to be controlled. They're taking no chances. If anyone talks, they'll expose us, and by inference, they will connect Mr. Roosevelt to the crime."

Jack Travers seemed stunned by Ethan's announcement. He sat quietly with everyone looking at him. "What's Angela's job? What's she supposed to do tonight?

Ethan mulled it over. "I think she's supposed to babysit the guy. Keep him focused. Make sure he doesn't chicken out. But she's going to end up right in the middle of everything."

"Who's holding her father?"

"I think he's being held by Yaras's bodyguard. They may be holed up in the attic of a house on 5th Street. It's Zangara's apartment."

"I know the guy you're talking about. Yaras called him Primo. I don't suppose that's his name, but he's as big as a house. And he packs a rod." Travers thought for a moment. "If we could grab her father, would Angela break free?"

"Sure. She doesn't want any part of this. She's just afraid for her father."

"But you know my deal with them. We can't interfere."

To Ethan, Travers's tone sounded bureaucratic. "Jack. She's just a kid, and she's afraid. She needs help. She could get hurt or go to jail. I want to help her. I really don't care about your deal. Even if she falls out of it, Zangara will still do the shooting. I know it."

"How would you know that, Ethan?" asked Travers.

"I just..."

Emma interceded. "Jack. Don't push him. Ethan has feelings for her. How would you like it if I was in her position? Let's do something. You never bargained for this. We can't be responsible for all this trouble."

Jack was quiet.

"Something has to be done, Jack. This whole thing is spiraling out of control," said Currant. "You know people, Jack. People who could save the old man. If he's in the clear, then so is Ethan's girl."

"You're right, A.C. Things are getting out of hand. But I can't involve my people. I might be able to work around your involvement. But to bring in anyone with authority...that will expose my position."

"Jack, I'm telling you," said Ethan, "everything could go bad. This Zangara guy is a nut. You made it sound like this was a professional hit. Like clockwork. Distasteful but clean-cut. I don't see that. We've got a mentally unstable guy led by a frightened young woman. What guarantee do we have that this guy will do the job?"

Travers stood. He walked over to the other side of the gazebo, sat on the railing, and looked back toward them. "You're right. He's not what I expected. But I know he won't be shooting at FDR. That's for sure."

"The man is under intense pressure, Jack. He's not some kind of cool-headed mechanic. He's in love. He's been sold a fantasy. He's got a gun to his head. Those five bullets he has could end up in anyone. Including FDR. You agree?"

"OK," said Travers. He looked down at the floor, almost mumbling the words. "You're right. Let's work something out. But no outsiders. This is our problem to solve."

Zak waved the group to attention. "Jack, we understand Mr. Roosevelt has bigger fish to fry than the battle between Cermak and the Outfit. These are tough times, and we're behind you. But you also have to trust us."

Jack smiled. "Thanks for the speech. Believe me. I

trust you. I just don't want any of you hurt."

They left the gazebo together and walked north along the water's edge. Ethan was getting nervous, not only for FDR but also for Angela. His feelings were a mess. She hadn't been entirely honest with him; he hadn't been honest with her either. No matter what, he wanted her to get away from Zangara. He said nothing as they walked. He wondered what Angela was doing at this moment.

Emma and Jack led, Zak and Ethan followed behind, and Dr. Currant brought up the rear. They walked along slowly, like soldiers on a death march, knowing that tragic events were about to unfold. If Jack was right, no harm would come to FDR. But Ethan knew the real story; he knew *The History*. FDR would die tonight.

"Ethan, you promised Angela you would stay near her tonight, right?" asked Travers.

"Yes."

"But can you promise me you won't interfere with Zangara?"

"I'm not going to touch him, Jack. But if we can find her father and get him to safety, I'll grab her. And I'm going to take her away, no matter whether you or Zangara or anyone else objects. If Joe Zangara has any real feelings for her, he's not going to want her there when he shoots. And whether she's there or not, he's going to do the deed. He's got no choice. But we can pull Angela out of this madness."

"And if we can't?"

Ethan gazed at the blue waters of Biscayne Bay, then back at Travers. "She's made up her mind. She won't do anything that would harm her father. But I'm still going to be there. If she needs my help, she'll get it. I'm going to watch over her. That's all I can do unless we pull her father out of the equation."

Emma jumped in. "Let Zak and me tackle that one, Jack. I think we can handle it."

Travers stopped in his tracks. They all stopped walking. "Are you crazy? I can't allow you to get anywhere near those mobsters, Emma. Absolutely not."

"You can't allow me?" she stammered. "I don't think it's as simple as that. I'm not your servant, Jack Travers."

Travers seemed flustered. "Emma, you know what I mean. I'm only concerned about you. Anyway, how could you and your voiceless friend take on an Outfit bodyguard? The guy has a gun. I saw it. And he's big. And you can't call in the cavalry. That could blow the whole deal."

Emma gave him a look. "How about listening to my idea before you reject the possibility? OK?"

"All right. But let's keep walking."

Jack and Emma walked ahead, but the others were close enough to hear their conversation.

"Zak and I can use your car. We can drive to Zangara's place and watch. We've got the rest of the day to wait for a break. Maybe that bodyguard will go out for cigarettes, maybe her father will escape, maybe they will move him somewhere else. I don't know, but it can't hurt to try. Don't worry. We won't do anything crazy. Do you want to come with us?"

Travers looked around and then looked back at Emma. "I can't. I can't be there. If Yaras sees me, he may forget about the deal. He has a mission too. And I'm sure he would just as well have a free hand in this matter. I don't want to give him any excuse."

"He may recognize Zak and me," she said.

"As far as I know, he's never seen either of you. But just don't give him an opportunity."

"Does that mean we can do it?" she asked with a smile.

"Hey, I'm not your boss, lady." Jack smiled. "You're a modern woman. Just be careful."

"Jack Travers..." she started to say something and then swallowed her words. "Don't worry. We'll be like two little mice. Right, Zak?"

Zak nodded and wrinkled his nose.

They turned and walked back to the hotel. To lower

their profile, they agreed to separate. Emma and Zak prepared to find Angela's father; Ethan told them he would talk to Angela to give her hope. And Jack suggested that he and Currant grab a drink.

"Now there's an idea," said Currant.

-Chapter XXI-

A Fly on the Wall

Zak and Emma gathered what they needed at the hotel and commandeered Jack Travers' 1930 Buick. Top up, rumble seat closed, Emma drove. Sitting in the passenger seat, Zak checked his watch: *2:37*. They had about six hours to get Angela's father away from Yaras. If they could do that, Angela would be free. Emma turned off Biscayne Boulevard onto 5th Street. She drove quickly through the commercial section, heading for Zangara's apartment.

Zak signed. *"Hey, take it easy. We don't want to get stopped for speeding."*

Emma slowed the car. In minutes, they were near the house. The street was lined with small warehouses, some stores, and a scattering of houses. Zangara's place was on the left side of the road. They inspected it as they drove by. No one was visible, and the driveway was empty.

"We'll go up a couple of blocks and then turn around and come back. I want to park facing the house," she said, almost muttering.

"Close enough to see, but far enough not to be seen," signed Zak.

Emma watched his fingers talk as she drove. She caught every word. "Right."

They swung onto 4th Avenue, circled the block, drove back, and parked. Emma switched off the engine.

"Well, here we are. I don't see anything," signed Zak.

"We've got the right place. It's that one over there." She pointed. "The white one with all the vines. Upstairs."

"So you want to try to storm the Bastille?" asked Zak.

"I think not. I wouldn't want to take on that guy Primo, even with your considerable strength. Jack says he's a beast. Anyway, he has a gun. Instead, we'll have to rely on our little friends."

"Just kidding. Only Jack would think that we'd try something like that."

"I'm glad he didn't want to help us. We don't need him nosing around. And anyway, I don't think he cares whether Angela's father gets freed tonight or not."

"Jack may not care, but you care."

"I care about my brother. He's up to his fat neck in love with this woman. If we can save her father, it's better for everyone. Jack has a different agenda. He's playing it safe. He can't see the future like we can."

"It may look like we're interfering with the Outfit."

"Not the way we're going to do it. They'll just look incompetent. No mobster wants to admit that to his boss."

Zak looked at Emma and smiled.

"What are you smiling about?" she asked.

Zak shrugged and signed, *"I was just thinking it's nice to be working with you again."*

Emma gave him a look. "Let's get to work, partner."

"You want me to grab our eternal salvation?"

"Please do, Zakaroo."

He reached into the back deck and extracted a leather-bound book. The words *HOLY BIBLE* were inscribed in gold leaf on the cover. It appeared to be the real thing with red-painted page edges and colored ribbon bookmarks dangling out. In fact, it was a fancy container for their spy equipment. Zak held the case on his lap and slid open the clasp. Raising the cover, he examined the contents. Six translucent plastic tubes containing bugs were tightly fitted into foam protective material: two red, two blue, and two green. In addition, a controller nested in a shaped slot. The inside top cover of the book was carefully fitted with a flat-glass viewing screen.

They parked at an empty building with a *FOR RENT* sign taped inside the window glass. The location offered a good view of the house, shielded somewhat by an overgrown tangle of bushes and ivy in the parkway. Emma looked through the windshield. An open window in the attic apartment faced the street. Its curtains fluttered in the breeze, but sunlight reflecting off the window obscured the glass.

"That window in the front is our way in, Zak." She giggled. "I feel just like Jimmy Stewart in *Rear Window*, except I don't have a broken leg. Let me have the controller."

Zak removed the device and handed it to Emma.

"It's been a while, but this is like riding a bike. You never forget. All right. Let's launch a green one. We'll go right in that open window."

Zak pulled out one of the green plastic tubes. Carefully, he removed the tiny house fly drone and held it gently in the palm of his hand.

"Let's test the camera," she said. She pushed a button on the controller, and the viewing screen came to life. "Turn the screen so I can see it." Zak adjusted the screen. An image of the Buick's dashboard appeared. "Hold it higher." She saw her own face. "It's working. Let's take it for a ride."

Emma worked the joystick. The mechanical bug's wings came to life and hummed quietly. Slowly, it rose from Zak's hand. Working from the monitor, she guided it out the car's window. It took off, quickly covering the open space between them and the apartment. It rose above the top of the building. Even though the wind was light, it required some skill to maintain altitude and direction. "I've got the hang of it now," she said. "I'm going in."

A wind current caught the fly, and the curtain fluttered. Just in time, Emma backed it out for another try. The drone waited outside the window, hovering. When the curtains stilled, it darted into the void. "*You're in!*" signed Zak.

Emma scanned the room. Slowly, the fly peered from one corner of the bedroom to the other. A man was lying on a bed. "That must be Angela's father," she said. She circled the fly around the room, staying just below the ceiling. There was no one else there. For practice, she made the fly hang from the ceiling.

"What are you doing?" asked Zak.

"I just want to look like a harmless housefly. I'll sit here for a few seconds and then tour the rest of the place. Below, Angela's father, lying face-up on the bed, stared at the fly. Emma wondered whether he would detect anything. But his face revealed nothing.

She took off from the ceiling and headed for the door. She was pleased that the house structure seemed to offer no interference with the drone's controls. In the hallway, she looked right: a dead end with a door on the left. She brought the fly to rest on the wall across from the door. The drone had three cameras: one viewed forward, one upward with a fish-eye lens, and one downward. She had a view of a bathroom. It was empty. The fly changed direction and buzzed down the hall, staying close to the ceiling. She didn't want to be swatted by anyone. For a moment, she rested again on the ceiling.

The view from the fish-eye was expansive and revealed the entire room: an exterior door on the far side, a kitchenette on one side of that door, and a seating arrangement on the other. In the corner, Primo sat, wearing a sleeveless undershirt and smoking a cigar. His pendulous gut hung over his belt, and a nickel-plated gun protruded from his shoulder holster. He leaned over and adjusted the tuner of a table radio, then sunk back into the sofa. Emma switched on the audio, and the drone picked up tinny musical sounds received by the phony Bible. Primo looked directly at the fly. He appeared to see it but showed no interest.

She flew the drone down toward the door. It had a deadbolt lock. She couldn't tell if it was locked, but she noticed the window adjacent to the door was open. She flew back onto the ceiling. Primo drew down on his cigar and blew out the smoke upward. She was about to leave when Angela's father, Salvatore, entered the room. "How much longer?" he asked.

"Nap time over? Relax. I'll get you back home late tonight. Sit down. I'm listening to *Amos 'n' Andy*. You like them?"

"*Molto divertente*," replied Salvatore. "Have another?"

"Another what?"

"Another cigar."

"Sure. Here." He grabbed a cigar from his case on the table, handed it to the man, and lit it.

Sal took in the smoke and exhaled loudly. "Thanks. Nothin' like a good cigar. Say, you think my Angela is good?"

"Don't worry, Pop. She can handle herself."

"But, tonight. It is dangerous?"

"Forget it. It will all be over soon. Shh...I'm listening."

They stopped talking, and Emma did some fly-like maneuvers and then headed down the corridor, through the bedroom, and carefully out the open window.

Zak and Emma looked up at the house. Their little spy-fly was out in the open. Emma skillfully brought him back. One moment, the fly was suspended in midair outside Zak's window; the next moment, she dropped it into Zak's open hand.

"I'm thinking those two seem awful friendly."

"*Too friendly.*"

Emma was perplexed. The scene in the attic did not appear threatening. "Seems a bit weird. But we don't know anything about her father. Maybe he's just making the best of a bad situation."

Zak rolled his eyes. "*Very cozy. If you ask me.*"

"Whatever. We'll find out when we grab Angela's father. Now we're going in for the kill...or should I say the sleep? Blue tube, yellow dot, Robin!"

"*OK, Batman.*" Zak prepared the next drone.

"Be careful holding it unless you want to take a quick nap. This one will knock out a grown man for a least an hour."

Zak set the bug down. "*Does it have a camera?*"

"No. It's strictly built for action."

"How does it know who to bite?"

"It's activated by body heat. Once I push the go button, it will bite any living being within the space and give me a signal."

"Then it will just fly around looking for new victims?"

"When I deactivate its bite, it will automatically return. Simple but effective," she said. "When it's done the deed, both Primo and Angela's father will be in la-la land. You'll have to carry him out. Think you can handle him?"

"No problem. He looks to be about a hundred fifty pounds. I can do that standing on my head."

"All right. No time like the present. Get it ready."

Zak dumped the drone into his hand. *"What happens if Primo swats at it?"*

"It's programmed to avoid any attempts to hit it. It's even smarter than a real housefly. Did you see the little hole on the bottom? That's the biter. The drone has suction cup feet. It will quickly grip bare skin and fire an injection into the host. The dose acts quickly. Then it's off, flying again. Let's go. Ready?"

Zak nodded. She was about to launch the injection drone when Zak tapped her leg. She looked up. A black Dodge car approached. They both ducked down behind the dashboard. "It must be Dave Yaras." The car pulled into the driveway and parked out of their view. They heard a door slam. "Damn," she said. "Timing is everything."

-Chapter XXII

The Rough Riders

Jack Travers and A.C. Currant sat comfortably in the plush chairs of the hotel lounge at a small table in the back of the room. It was the middle of the afternoon, and only a few people shared the space. Officially, the hotel did not serve alcohol, but the management was not above providing everything but the booze and turning their collective heads aside, letting patrons do the rest. Prohibition was on its way out, and while not officially dead, most people celebrated its upcoming demise, unconcerned with legalities. Jack ordered two Coca-Colas, and he increased the pleasure of the drinks with a couple of shots from his personal flask. In the background, a radio announcer mentioned the impending visit of Franklin Roosevelt. This seemed to spur the conversation of people in the room. The waiter checked in, but Travers waved him off. A.C. Currant lazily sipped his drink. Not exactly Johnnie Walker Black, but it would do. He gazed out the window at the traffic on Biscayne Boulevard.

"A few more hours and 'whatever will be, will be,' Jack." He turned to look at Travers as he spoke. "I'll be glad when it's all over. I'm not getting any younger, you know."

Jack Travers wore a severe look. "There's a complication, A.C."

"Life is full of them, Jack."

"Yes, but I'm afraid of this one. I know Emma and her brother think I'm cold-blooded regarding Cermak. But they're a bit naive. Cermak made his own bed. My biggest concern is for others...not just our people, but innocent bystanders. Ethan is right about Zangara. The man's under pressure. He could just as easily miss

Cermak and fire into the crowd."

Currant nodded. "That's something you'll have to learn to deal with, Jack. If you don't want to make waves...you can't control it. That's your game plan, right?"

Travers lit a cigarette. He looked around the room. "I'm certainly not running this show. And my bosses aren't even involved. But I can see the future. I know something terrible will happen, but I can't do anything to stop it."

"Having second thoughts?"

Jack looked at his watch. "I was hoping the Outfit might blow its cover and make its attempt sooner. Someplace else. Then Roosevelt's security guys would cancel the speech, and no one would get hurt."

Currant raised his eyebrows. "Except Cermak."

"Right. That's a given. Whether here and now or someplace else and later, the mayor's time has expired." He took a drag from his cigarette and exhaled heavily as he sunk back into the chair.

Currant could see that the uncertainty was getting to Jack. "You can't save anyone except for those around you, Jack. Keep my niece and nephew out of the fray. Keep Zak out of the action. Maybe we can get Angela away from Zangara. Maybe Emma and Zak will find a way to free the old man."

"That's a long shot. I don't even know why I let her try to find him."

"Don't worry about Emma. Unlike her brother, she won't take any unnecessary risks."

Travers looked directly at him. "I appreciate your insight, A.C." He slid his finger between his neck and collar. "I hope you're right."

"Don't worry. I know I am." He smiled. "Another drink?"

"No. One's enough. We have to stay sharp."

Currant looked out the window. In the distance, gray clouds were forming. Roosevelt was at sea on Astor's yacht. They would be heading for Miami soon. Maybe the president-elect was sharing a drink with his rich and powerful friends. Was he aware of the danger ahead? Or was he thinking about catching another fish? He wondered what it was like to be an aristocrat, free of all the concerns of the common man: the wanting for food, shelter, a job. The Great Depression probably meant little to the Astors, the DuPonts, the Rockefellers, and the Roosevelts. They're sport fishing while everyone else is scratching out a meager existence.

Of course, unlike the other chosen people, fate had given Franklin Roosevelt a solid taste of reality. His illness weighed on him as profoundly as any of the misfortunes of the common man. Roosevelt had joined the ranks of the everyman when polio destroyed the use of his legs and created a jumble of other physical and mental problems. It had to be humbling to this man of the upper class. When you have no control over your bowels, thought Currant, you're no longer one of the chosen. FDR would probably have traded his position for the luxury of taking a peaceful shit at his leisure. He drifted back to Jack Travers, the man responsible for keeping FDR alive today.

"Jack, relax. Why don't we have another? FDR has plenty of bodyguards. That's not our assignment. You've done your job. Have a drink and call it a day. Keep the kids safe. What else can you do?"

"I'm afraid I have some additional news about tonight, A.C." He swallowed hard and snuffed out his cigarette in the ashtray. He looked around. His voice was hushed now. "There will be another shooter tonight. Someone who is out to get Roosevelt and Roosevelt alone."

Currant followed his cue. No one appeared interested in their conversation. But nevertheless, he too dropped his volume. "Another shooter? But Zangara is the shooter."

"He is, but he won't shoot at FDR. Another shooter has been hired to kill Franklin Roosevelt."

This was all news to Currant, and he was someone

who knew the future: Zangara killed Franklin Roosevelt. It was all over *The History*. There was no other shooter. If there was a different shooter who intended to kill Roosevelt, Jack's agreement with the Outfit would not be enough. "How do you know? Who's this shooter?"

"I don't know. And I can't reveal my source, but I know. It's a fact. I have reliable information. They're going to use Zangara as cover. Everyone will be focusing on the little Italian firing, and no one will see the real shooter. It's a perfect plan. I'm telling you, and you alone, A.C., because I want you to help me stop this attack."

Currant was more than puzzled; he was almost lost for words. "Why don't you...why don't you just inform the Secret Service?"

"Because, if they know, they will cancel the event. Cermak will live. And our friends in Chicago won't be pleased. That's just the trouble I was supposed to eliminate."

"How about after Roosevelt arrives? Tell somebody then so they can be on the lookout."

Travers shook his head. "If I go up to one of the security people and start giving them directions, they'll probably lock me up."

"But you work for him."

"I work for Mrs. Roosevelt. I've got business cards. Anyone can make up business cards. I'm in the background. Deep in the background."

"But if you have all this information. All these details. They must come from someone on top...."

"Forget that. I'm in a box. I'm walled in by my own creations. But you and I are going to stop this person. I know that whoever is behind all this is not taking chances. They want a direct shot from close range. And unlike Zangara, the new shooter will be a professional."

"What can we do?" asked Currant.

"All we can do is get close enough to follow the action. Roosevelt's car will drive in on the road between the stage and the crowd. The car will stop in front of the stage. He'll speak from the backseat of his automobile, using a microphone. A short speech. It will be late at night, and he'll be tired. A few words and that will be that. Zangara will position himself to get Cermak, who will be on the stage. We only have to watch Zangara; the real shooter will be opposite him. If he's on the left, our guy will be on the right, or vice versa. We have to follow Zangara very closely. Maybe Angela will be with him, maybe she won't. But if we track him and properly position ourselves, we might have a chance at stopping the shooter."

"How?" This was all starting to look impossible, thought Currant.

"We must get close enough to tackle him, grab his arm, or knock him down. This guy will be focused. Not looking for someone to stop him. He's going to wait for Zangara's first shot. Then he'll fire. It will all happen in a few seconds. If we knock him out of the way before he can shoot, his window of opportunity will close. He needs to blend in with Zangara's shots. He can't fire after that. Anyway, the Secret Service will drape their bodies over FDR as soon as they hear the shots. It's a split-second window. Once it's closed, it's closed."

"Jack, I'm an old man," said Currant.

Travers smiled and scoffed. "A.C. Currant. You're a Rough Rider."

Currant absorbed the compliment, cocked his head to the side, and rolled his eyes, looking to the heavens, thinking that the world would be better off if he controlled his chronic need to impress other people with exaggerations or, worse, flat-out lies. He looked his lie in the face and weakly replied, "Right, Jack. Bully. Bully for us!"

-Chapter XXIII-

Bedtime for Bonzo

"What time is it?" asked Emma. Zak showed her the face of his watch...*8:00*. The sun was low in the sky, and the trees now cast long shadows. The waiting had been frustrating and unanticipated. Emma was about to give up the whole project. The only recent activity had happened at about six o'clock. A man entered the front door of the house on the first floor. They assumed he was the owner of the house. But Yaras, who had entered the attic apartment hours ago, had not been seen again. She and Zak had taken turns watching. One of them would go for a short walk every half hour, stop at a nearby gasoline station, grab a soda, sometimes use the washroom, and return, always hoping that Dave Yaras would be gone. But it was not to be. Yaras's flashy black Dodge sedan remained in the driveway, and there was no sign of Zangara.

"This is getting boring," signed Zak. *"I thought for sure we'd be back at the rally by this time, handing off Angela's father and taking a bow for our trouble."*

"I'm with you there, Zak. Should we go?"

"Let's give it another half hour. If he doesn't leave by then, it's a waste of time. OK?"

"Sounds like a plan."

Each minute, the fading light crept nearer to total darkness, and Emma wondered if she would be able to navigate the drone. She would have to get it through the window. The biting drones had only one camera. But they were equipped with night vision if necessary. At the moment, the bedroom that held Angela's father was dark. She couldn't see if there were any lights on in the living room. They waited.

Fifteen minutes later, they got a break. A door

slammed, the car started, and the Dodge whined as it rolled out of the driveway in reverse. They ducked again, but Yaras paid no attention to them. In seconds, he was on his way downtown.

"Let's go," said Emma. "The blue one with the yellow dot on the tube."

"Sleep bite?"

"Normal-light camera, sleep bite," she said.

"What are these red ones?"

"Currant said those shouldn't be used. Hit-man stuff."

"Got it," signed Zak. He removed the bug from the tube. It rested in his hand.

"Just enough light to find our way. Hey, wait! The light in the bedroom is on now. This will be easy." With the controller in her hand, she fired up the fly. Its wings buzzed softly. Zak looked nervous. "Don't worry. I won't push the wrong button, Zak." The drone lifted off. She guided it out the window, and then it disappeared. They tracked its progress on the monitor as it headed for the bright light of the open window. Once inside, she activated it. "Bedtime for Bonzo!" she said.

Zak looked puzzled. *"Say what?"*

"It's an old '50s movie. About a chimpanzee named Bonzo with Ronald Reagan."

"Who?"

"Forget it. Check your watch. We'll let it do its magic. In ten minutes, we're going in."

Zak watched the Buick's dashboard clock. At ten minutes, he snapped his fingers. They both shot out of the car and ran down the walk and up the driveway. For a moment, they hesitated at the top landing. *"Did you deactivate that thing? I don't want this to be bedtime for Zakaroo."*

Zak tried the door; it was locked. He reached in through the adjacent open window. Soon, the deadbolt clicked. They opened the door and entered. Primo was half-sitting, half-laying on the sofa—out cold.

"Move him into a sleeping position, Zak. He's going to be the stooge. He'll think he just fell asleep on his own when he wakes up."

"What about bite marks?" Zak asked.

"A tiny, almost invisible ankle bite."

Zak walked over to Primo and gave him a shove. He fell into place on the sofa without so much as a grunt. Carefully, Zak arranged the guard's body. *"Where's the bug?"*

"Right here. Came back to me like a faithful dog." She handed it to Zak, who returned it to the tube, capped it, and stuffed it into his shirt pocket. "Let's get papa and get out of here."

The old man was stretched out on the bed, looking weak and frail. Zak wasted no time. He bent over and lifted the man, cradling him like a child. Emma stood behind him and cleared the way out. As she opened the front door, Zak swung the body through, avoiding the doorframe. He was halfway down the steps when she closed the door behind her.

In seconds, he reached the car, placed the man into the front seat, and closed the door gently. He looked around, but no one else was on the street. Emma followed, got in, and started the car. Zak looked at his watch. He put his arm through the passenger side window for Emma to see. It was *8:45.* Roosevelt would arrive at Bayfront Park in about a half-hour.

"Get in!" she said. Zak straightened up their sleeping passenger and leaned Sal's head onto Emma's shoulder. Then he went around the back of the car, opened the rumble seat, and climbed in. When Emma heard his knock on the roof, she took off. The comatose man beside her slid away. She grabbed him with her free hand and pulled him back. "Hold on, Poppy. We'll have you there in a few minutes."

-Chapter XXIV-

Shadows in the Dark

That hot fateful night, red, white, and blue lights cast an eerie and surrealistic glow on the array of palm trees surrounding the outdoor amphitheater. Ethan surveyed the crowd looking for an answer, searching for some way to stop the impending carnage. But the place was a mob scene, filled with more people than he had ever imagined would attend the rally. Tens of thousands massed together, forming a human oven that grew hotter every minute. An anxious murmur of anticipation filled the sticky air as the citizens of Miami swatted insects and nervously chattered while waiting in the heat. A drum and bugle corps played loudly, further stirring the emotions of the excited and impatient crowd. Maybe a third of those gathered were seated; the others stood shoulder to shoulder, jostling for a peek at the new president.

Ethan stood at the rear. Earlier, he watched Giuseppe Zangara and Angela as they struggled to make their way to the front of the crowd. Zangara was positioned to the left of center stage. His target, Anton Cermak, sat with many others on the elevated platform. Ethan's height and Angela's bright yellow clothing allowed him to easily track them. Roosevelt was running late but was due at any moment.

Ethan checked behind him, hoping to see Emma and Zak, with or without Salvatore Marra. Hours ago, they left to scout out Zangara's apartment. Since then, he had not heard from them, and the rally site was now inaccessible by car. The police were not letting any vehicles enter the parking area as they cleared the entry road for Roosevelt's arrival. He looked across a surging sea of heads. He found Angela's hat in the glow of light from the brightly illuminated platform. The strange couple, the little man and the girl in the yellow dress, was moving closer to the roadway and nearer to their quarry. Ethan stood in the darkness, surrounded by sweating people.

When floodlights on the roof of the building ignited, illuminating the entire roadway area in front of the stage, the crowd was momentarily silenced. Ethan could still make out the yellow bonnet, but the ring of light only extended to the front row of well-wishers gathered across the roadway. Everyone else waited in the dark. It was the perfect setting for an assassination. Ethan knew that under these conditions, anything was possible. There was no way that bodyguards and police could stop an assassin from killing FDR.

A.C. Currant and Jack Travers made it to the front. Jack showed his credentials to a city cop attempting to control the crowd. After one look, the officer immediately waved them ahead into a grassy area in front of the first row of seating. Nearby others were sitting and lying on the grass like it was a picnic. Without hesitation, Currant walked across the road and positioned himself. He looked up at the special guests on the stage. All were dressed for the occasion, the women in expensive outfits and the men in fine linen suits. Currant spotted Cermak sitting in the front row of the onstage dignitaries. The mayor was talking to another man, and on either side sat two men looking out of place. Their cheap wool suits betrayed them as bodyguards. He looked around. On the ground, at the far end of the stage, stood a uniformed policeman who watched the crowd closely. Three other men in cold-weather suits stood near Cermak on the ground below the platform, spaced about ten feet apart.

Currant looked back across the road. Travers stood motionless, his eyes scanning for trouble. For a moment, they locked onto each other. Travers nodded as if to approve Currant's position.

There were a few people in the area that Currant now

guarded. They looked like guests; maybe they were latecomers. The area behind Currant was cordoned off, and a security guard verified the guest invitations and restricted admissions. Another cop passed through security and headed toward A.C. This pleased him as he was concerned that he might be the last line of defense in this area. Tensions rose, and the aging physicist reached into his pants pocket and gripped the device. In his state of agitation, simply touching it comforted him. Sweating, uptight, and anxious, hc wantcd to make a difference and fix the future. But now, caught in the middle of this historical moment, he wanted to be anywhere else. The milling sounds of the throng increased. Ahead something was happening. Currant jumped up and down, and in the distance, he saw headlights. The new American leader was coming.

Dave Yaras had circled the stage building. From a position in the back, he spotted Three Fingers Jack White standing next to the stage, wearing gloves to hide his missing fingers. Dressed in the Cicero police uniform with a badge, White looked official. So far, so good. Yaras searched the crowd. The faces of the people were brightly illuminated. He caught sight of Angela's yellow dress. Zangara was at her side. Although Frankie Rio wasn't visible. Yaras knew if he could find Zangara, so could Rio. With his crew in place, he walked around the back of the building, nodded to the security guard checking invitations, and walked toward the entry road. There was only one person in that area, an older man. To his far left stood a group of four people. Two of them appeared to be holding some kind of sign. He decided to stay well away from the road until the moment came. Instinctively, to reassure himself, he tapped the leather of his sidearm holster. A slight bulge in his front pocket revealed the tubular silencer mechanism. He glanced at it. Everything was in place. The crowd noise increased. The band struck up "Hail to the Chief" as Yaras edged closer.

Emma and Zak were frustrated. The Buick was stalled in traffic. The police had directed all vehicles to the curb, and their car couldn't move. They sat in front of their hotel, about two blocks from the rally. After about five minutes, Zak got out of the rumble seat and stepped to the driver's side door. *"Forget it. I'll grab the old man and take him in."*

Emma looked at Salvatore Marra. Angela's father sat beside her, still half-asleep. She looked back at Zak. "OK. Give it a shot. Roosevelt has to be coming. The place is on lockdown."

Zak needed no more encouragement. He circled the front of the car and opened the passenger side door. He beckoned the man to come out. The old man appeared to be lost. He mumbled something in Italian and looked at Emma plaintively.

"It's OK, Mr. Marra. Zak will take you to Angela. Please go now. You must hurry!"

"Angela?" He mumbled her name as if she were in a dream. His head dropped again to Emma's shoulder.

Zak couldn't wait. He reached in, rudely pulled Marra out of the car, and guided him to the curb. As they avoided cars and stumbled slowly across Biscayne Boulevard, Zak checked the route to the brightly illuminated amphitheater. In the shadows in front of this stark backdrop, he watched the three cars of the Roosevelt entourage slowly travel along the access road with masses of spectators and well-wishers waving at either side. The band played. Time was running out. He grabbed Salvatore Marra, lifted him like a child, and carried him. Considering his load, he moved swiftly in the darkness, avoiding people and trees.

Ethan watched Angela's hat bob up and down in the distance. The Roosevelt cars had pulled in front of the stage area. The crowd screamed in delight. The band continued to play. For a moment, he thought he saw A.C. Currant standing on the other side of the road to the right of the stage. He had no idea why he would be there, and he dismissed the thought. He looked around for Zak or Emma, but saw neither. He felt helpless. He was far away from Angela, and she was in harm's way. He debated whether to force his way through the crowd to pull her away from danger, but he knew she would resist. He needed her father, and he needed him now.

The sound system in the park came alive. The band stopped playing, and the announcer gave the introduction. Ethan, much taller than anyone in the crowd, could see that Roosevelt was dressed in a dark suit and hatless. His familiar pince-nez glasses reflected the spotlights illuminating the scene. The President-elect looked tall and imposing as he sat atop the rear deck of his car.

FDR turned to face the crowd. A large smile graced his face. He waved before speaking. "Mr. Mayor, my friends of Miami...." There was a wild burst of applause and cheers from the audience. He waited for the din to recede.

"I am not a stranger here because for a good many years, I used to come down here. I have not been here for seven years, but I am coming back, for I have firmly resolved not to make this the last time. I have had a very wonderful twelve days fishing in these Florida and Bahama waters. It has been a splendid rest, and we have caught a great many fish, but I am not going to attempt to tell you any fishing stories." The audience laughed and applauded.

"The only fly in the ointment on my trip has been that I have put on about ten pounds, so that means that among the other duties that I shall have to perform when I get up north is taking those ten pounds off." More laughter and applause followed. "I hope very much to be able to come down here next winter, and to see all of you, and to have another enjoyable ten days or two weeks in Florida waters. Many thanks."

The speech everyone had gathered together to hear had been heard, but the cheering and screaming continued unabated. The band played again.

Immediately after finishing his speech, with the help of others, Roosevelt was moved into the backseat. The car was quickly surrounded by people stepping down from the stage to greet Roosevelt. Ethan believed the heavyset man wearing a dark suit and eyeglasses who approached the vehicle was Mayor Anton Cermak. The two men spoke for a few seconds. Cermak smiled, shook FDR's hand, and then turned away.

Ethan felt a tug on his jacket. He turned to face Zak and spotted Angela's father. He was elated. He gave Zak a thumbs-up and hugged the man. "Come with me. We must save Angela now!" he shouted. Salvatore Marra seemed confused. Ethan dragged him forward into the crowd. Soon Marra moved quicker as if he had some instinctive understanding that his daughter was in trouble. The two struggled to make headway through the mass of bodies.

A.C. Currant was only about fifteen feet from Franklin Roosevelt. The speech was completed, and the area was crazy with people. Currant saw Mayor Cermak near Roosevelt's car. Crossing Currant's field of vision, a man cleared the way for two people carrying a long sign. Later, he would be told that the banner was an oversized telegram welcoming Roosevelt to Miami. But at the moment, it was confusing. Two men held the sign up for FDR to see. The policeman standing a few feet to the left of Currant moved directly behind the sign. Currant assumed he was about to chase these men away.

Ethan and Salvatore Marra struggled to move through the crowd. Ethan was almost maniacal now. He tossed people to the side who would not let them through. He saw Angela about fifteen feet distant. Zangara was in front of her. Ethan yelled her name. She didn't react. He cried out again, "Angela. Come here. Your father is here!"

She backed away from Zangara; she must have heard

Ethan's voice. She looked distraught as she turned, seeming to recognize both of them. Ethan got within a few feet of her. Her eyes were cold. "Go away, you fool. Leave me alone!" she yelled.

Ethan struggled with her words. "But we've got your father. Come with me now!"

"Stay out of this. Get him out of here. Go away, Ethan!"

The surging crowd pushed Ethan back. Angela helped Zangara balance as he climbed atop an empty metal chair. Now the little man could see over the heads of people. He had the revolver in his hand. He aimed, and the gun fired five quick shots. The people nearby cried out. Others were unaware of what had happened.

On the other side of the road, Currant watched in surprised horror as the uniformed policeman standing in front of him pulled his gun from his holster and pointed it toward FDR. The man had a clear shot over the telegram sign. Currant was slow to react, but he did. He reached into his pocket and pulled out the device. With two steps, he found his target. He placed the electrodes of the weapon directly onto Dave Yaras's bare neck as he squeezed the trigger. Only Currant heard the buzzing sound. Yaras fell limp, but Currant maintained the electrical contact on his neck. Shots were fired by others, but Yaras could not react. He was down for the count.

As Zangara emptied his revolver, Ethan ignored him in the rush of excitement. He was totally focused on Angela. One second, she was smiling, not at Ethan but at Zangara. She wore an almost gleeful look. The next second, her face went blank, and she fell to the ground. Frankie Rio had fired at Zangara. He missed, and his bullet struck Angela. She went down. Panicked, escaping people stepped on her body as they ran away from the gunshots. A crush of men, some police and some not, rushed at Zangara and knocked him to the ground. Once subdued, they helped him up while many in the crazed crowd, like animals, pawed at him, stripping him of almost all his clothes. They dragged the assassin out. Ethan fought his way to Angela. He knelt next to her and cradled her in his arms. The feet and legs of others bounced off of him. He shouted at them and swung his fists, crying in anguish and frustration. He looked down at her, and her eyes seemed to know him for a moment. Then they closed. "Angela..." He kissed her gently on the lips. She was warm but dead.

Currant lifted himself off of Yaras's body and pocketed his stun device. He looked down at the man and then stepped back. Yaras was stirring. Roosevelt's car was moving slowly toward Currant. He caught a glimpse of FDR and heard the President-elect tell his driver to stop. His voice was strong, and his command undeniable. Roosevelt was alive and well, directing others to help the wounded Mayor of Chicago. Quickly, Currant scanned the area, searching for Jack Travers, but Travers found him first.

Jack put his lips close to Currant's right ear. "Let's get out of here, now."

Zak was pummeled by the raging emotions of the crowd, yet he forced himself to remain focused. If not, he would be swept away by the intensity of his feelings. He caught up to Ethan and found him bent over his love, sobbing. Angela's father also wept beside his daughter. Zak didn't know what had happened, but he knew that his friends could not be made a part of this historical moment. He pulled Ethan away from Angela and grabbed her body. Ethan reached out for him, but Zak was too quick.

He carried Angela's lifeless body over his shoulder and ran into the night, searching for Emma. When he found her, he placed the body in the front seat of the Buick. They drove away. Zak looked back and saw a receding image of Ethan standing near the curb, watching them, looking terribly lost.

Emma drove north fast, heading for the hospital. Zak perched in the rumble seat gazed dimly at the police cars and ambulances screaming past, heading for Bayfront Park. At this moment, he dissolved. Silently, he cried hard. Tears slid down his cheeks, drifted away, and disappeared into the salty air of the warm night.

LOG of Zak Newman
February 19, 1933 (local time): 23:10 (Day 17 of time travel)

These last three days have been rough. That night, during our wild ride, Emma checked Angela for signs of life. There were none. Somehow Emma found Jackson Hospital by following an ambulance. When we arrived, it was a medical madhouse. Other shooting victims were carried in, including Mayor Cermak. The hospital staff pulled Angela out of the car. We told them she was hit while watching the Roosevelt rally. They took her body into the hospital. There were many shots fired that night, and every bullet must have hit at least one person. In the hospital confusion, we drifted away, but not before actually seeing Franklin Delano Roosevelt.

After the shooting, rather than rush away, Roosevelt had told his driver to wait. He demanded that the wounded Cermak be placed in his car. The two men were driven to the hospital. And right before our eyes, Roosevelt, sitting in a wheelchair, rolled into the admitting area, pushed by a Secret Service man. He looked good. Uninjured, tanned, and barking orders like a traffic cop. He was quite impressive.

We had done what we could, and we got out of there before anyone started asking questions about us. The next day, Jack Travers placed a call to Nitti's lawyer in Chicago. He demanded that the man contact his client and arrange for Angela's wake and burial. Nitti must have seen the benefit of controlling the body and any probing questions about her and her relationship to Dave Yaras. While the death of Angela was tragic, her send-off was well orchestrated by the funeral home. Nitti spared no expense. All of us attended, paid our respects, and then quietly left the scene. Ethan made it through the funeral and burial. He hasn't said much since the shooting. Of course, he was shaken by Angela's death, but something else is gnawing at him. I can tell. When I asked him about it, he clammed up. He only said one thing. "It wasn't real." When I asked him to explain, he just looked at me sadly and said, "I don't know anything. I've been a fool." I'm sure he'll explain later. But I'm leaving him alone for the moment.

We're checking out tomorrow. Emma, Ethan, A.C. Currant, and I will be boarding a northbound train. Jack Travers will drive back to Washington, D.C., alone.

Emma is coming back with us. No matter what, we have accomplished that, and FDR is alive.

End 02-19-33

-Chapter XXV-

Time Out

Emma and Jack took one last walk. They headed for Biscayne Bay, turning away from the band shell area when they reached the water's edge. They had no interest in reliving last Wednesday's tragic events. They walked north, where the water was protected and calm. A few pleasure boats skittered about the bay, noisy gulls floated above, and a breeze drifted in. It was a warm, perfect Florida day. Other lovers taking this walk might have found it ideal. But for Emma and Jack, it only brought the sadness of parting. Beneath a cluster of palm trees, they stopped and kissed as if they would never kiss again. They pulled apart, hand in hand, drifted along, each knowing this might be the last time they would be together. Emma had already informed Jack that she was going home. He said he understood. Both knew that these were only words. In her heart, she knew she would only regret leaving Jack.

Emma wanted to break the spell of melancholy that walked with them. "What will you tell Mrs. Roosevelt?" she asked.

Jack thought. "Oh. I hadn't thought about it. But I'm sure I'll just give her the basics. The less she knows, the better. From her perspective, all is well. She will know nothing about Angela or the details of the attacks. We are the only people who will know about the other shooter. And only I know who that shooter was. And I'm not telling."

"Secrets, eh?"

Jack smiled. "That's the way it is in Washington. Some things are best left unknown. It's much easier for honest, good-hearted people who live in the limelight to be blissfully unaware. Then there will be no painful lying. The story of the attempted assassination will only reveal a part of the truth. Enough to satisfy those who could not possibly accept the real truth. The story bubbling to the surface will describe Giuseppe Zangara as a disgruntled Italian immigrant who wanted to kill all the kings and presidents. Why?" He shrugged his shoulders. "People will invent a reason. But for certain, there will be no acknowledgment of the obvious."

"You mean that Cermak was shot by the Outfit?"

"Right. I understand Zangara is already blaming his actions on his terrible stomach pains. Maybe he thinks that's some kind of defense, or he was told to say that. So far, only Angela has died. I don't know who shot her. And there's been no hint of that in any news report. Somehow Nitti appears to have scrubbed the hospital records clean."

"So Zangara won't be up for a murder charge?"

"Either way, he'll be in for a life sentence. But there were many people wounded. I understand one of them is in serious condition. If anyone dies, Zangara will be executed."

"What about Mayor Cermak?"

"I heard he's coming around. He may live."

"The street war continues," she said.

"For certain." Jack took a deep breath. "But will we?"

"Will we what?"

"Continue."

She released his hand, put her arms around him, and held him tight. They looked into each other's souls. There was a long moment of silence before she spoke. "Don't worry. I'm coming back, my love. No matter what, I'm coming back. I don't know when...."

He held her tighter. "Emma, I have to tell you something about me that will change all of our lives forever." Then he spoke just a few words before Emma stopped him.

"Jack, I don't want to know."

"You must," he said. And he explained everything.

LOG of Zak Newman
February 25, 2033 (local time): 11:20

We are all back in time. Emma has a lot of explaining to do about her romantic situation and the future. I feel she's about to reveal something big, but for the moment, she's just settling back into the future. Mr. Wright happy to have his "little girl" back.

Ethan has pretty much been in seclusion. I don't blame him. He is shaken.

Dr. Currant is concerned that our travels may have been monitored. He's investigating this ominous possibility.

And this morning, I checked out my copy of The History. *I just wanted to see what happened to all those people we came into contact with on our journey. As expected, they are all dead.*

- *Anton Cermak, Mayor of Chicago, murdered, died March 6, 1933, of wounds received on February 15, 1933, age 59*
- *Giuseppe (Joe) Zangara, executed in electric chair, died March 20, 1933, age 33*
- *Three Fingers Jack White, murdered, died January 23, 1934, age 34*
- *Frankie Rio, heart attack, died February 23, 1935, age 40*
- *Frank Nitti, suicide, died March 19, 1943, age 57*
- *Saul Alinsky, heart attack, died June 12, 1962, age 63*
- *Dave Yaras, murdered?/heart attack?, died 1974, age 62*

I was going to check about the Roosevelts' lives, but I'll wait until tomorrow. For the moment, I'll leave myself guessing about the success of our mission in 1933. I must say, as I look out the window, everything pretty much looks the same. I hope not.

End 02-25-2033

—THE END—

TIME TRAVEL TWINS

W. Green

SAVING JFK
Volume 1

The Twins attempt to stop the Chicago

assassination of JFK in November 1963,

and create a better future for

their world of 2028.

X-OOMING FDR
Volumes 2, 3, 4

Determined to redesign history and the

life of a man who is only a footnote in the

history books of the 21st century, the Twins

travel into danger and intrigue.

SAVING TRUMP
Volume 5

The year is 2016, and the Twins and Zak

team up with their descendants, Samantha and

Jason Keene, during the presidential election.

Donald Trump is in…but does he continue?

BOOKS BY OTHERS RELATED TO THE EVENTS DESCRIBED IN X-ooming *FDR*

The Bonus Army: An American Epic by Paul Dickson
and Thomas B. Allen.
Published by Walker & Company, 2004.

War is a Racket by Major General Smedley Butler.
Published by World Classics Books, 2010.

Since Yesterday: 1929-1939 by Frederick Lewis Allen.
Published by Bantam Books, 1961.

B. E. F.: The Whole Story Of The Bonus Army by W.W.
Waters and William C. White. Published by Cincinnatus
Press, 2007.

The Last of the Doughboys: The Forgotten Generation
and Their Forgotten World War by Richard Rubin.
Published by Houghton Mifflin Harcourt, 2013.

The Five Weeks of Giuseppe Zangara: The Man Who
Would Assassinate FDR by Blaise Picchi. Published by
Academy Chicago Publishers, 1998.

The Outfit: The Role of Chicago's Underworld in the
Shaping of Modern America by Gus Russo. Published by
Bloomsbury, 2001.

Since Yesterday: 1929-1939 by Frederick Lewis Allen.
Published by Bantam Books, 1965.

The Plots Against the President by Sally Denton.
Published by Bloomsbury Press, 2012.

The Chicago Outfit by John J. Binder. Published by
Arcadia Publishing, 2003.

<u>When Capone's Mob Murdered Roger Touhy</u> by John W. Tuohy. Published by Barricade Books Inc., 2001.

<u>Florida in the Great Depression</u> by Nick Wynne & Joseph Knetsch. Published by The History Press, 2012,

<u>The Plot to Seize the White House</u> by Jules Archer. Published by Skyhorse Publishing, 2007.

<u>It Can't Happen Here</u> by Sinclair Lewis. Published by New America Library, 2005.

<u>FDR's Deadly Secret</u> by Steven Lomazow, M.D. and Eric Fettmann, Public Affairs, 2009.

<u>Devil Dog: The Amazing True Story of the Man Who Saved America</u> by David Talbot with Illustrations by Spain Rodriguez. Published by Simon & Schuster, 2010.

Thanks for Reading

X-ooming FDR 1933

Did you like the book? Your on-line book review will really help the author get the word out.